Bello:

hidden talent rediscovered

GW00854456

Bello is a digital only imprint of Pan Macmillan,
established to breathe new life into previously published,
classic books.

At Bello we believe in the timeless power of the imagination,
of good story, narrative and entertainment and we want to use
digital technology to ensure that many more readers
can enjoy these books into the future.

We publish in ebook and Print on Demand formats
to bring these wonderful books to new audiences.

About Bello:

www.panmacmillan.com/bello

Sign up to our newsletter to hear about
new releases, events and competitions:

www.panmacmillan.com/bellonews

B E L L O

Nina Bawden

1925 . 2 ... 12   PPE

Nina Bawden was one of Britain's most distinguished and best-loved novelists for both adults and young people. Several of her novels for children – *Carrie's War*, a Phoenix Award winner in 1993; *The Peppermint Pig*, which won the Guardian Fiction Award; *The Runaway Summer*; and *Keeping Henry* – have become contemporary classics.

She wrote over forty novels, slightly more than half of which are for adults, an autobiography and a memoir describing her experiences during and following the Potters Bar rail crash in May 2002, which killed her husband, Austen Kark, and from which she emerged seriously injured – but fighting. She was shortlisted for the 1987 Man Booker Prize for *Circles of Deceit* and several of her books, like *Family Money* (1991), have been adapted for film or television. Many of her works have been translated into numerous languages.

Born in London in 1925, Nina studied Philosophy, Politics and Economics at Oxford University in the same year as Margaret Thatcher. Following Potter's Bar, she was movingly portrayed as a character in the David Hare play, *The Permanent Way*, about the privatization of the British railways. She received the prestigious S T Dupont Golden Pen Award for a lifetime's contribution to literature in 2004, and in 2010 *The Birds on the Trees* was shortlisted for the Lost Booker of 1970.

Nina Bawden

CHANGE HERE
FOR BABYLON

BELL⦿

First published in 1955 by Collins

This edition published 2012 by Bello
an imprint of Pan Macmillan, a division of Macmillan Publishers Limited
Pan Macmillan, 20 New Wharf Road, London N1 9RR
Basingstoke and Oxford
Associated companies throughout the world

www.panmacmillan.com/imprints/bello
www.curtisbrown.co.uk

ISBN 978-1-4472-3590-3 EPUB
ISBN 978-1-4472-3589-7 POD

Visit **www.panmacmillan.com** to read more about all our books
and to buy them. You will also find features, author interviews and
news of any author events, and you can sign up for e-newsletters
so that you're always first to hear about our new releases.

Chapter One

The execution took place on a mild day, early in February. It had been raining during the night and the pavements steamed in the moist, morning sun. It was gentle weather; the soft sky held the promise of spring and not the retribution of winter. When it was over, they posted a notice on the gates of the prison and the people jostled each other to be the first to read it. They were mostly women and they talked in hushed whispers as though they were in church. A stray dog snuffled in the dirty gutters and a little boy in wellington boots wailed on a long, persistent note and tugged at his mother's sleeve. There was no triumphant sense of justice done, only bewildered appraisal of an uncomprehended act. It was a messy way to die.

I waited for a little while although there was no point in waiting. Then I went home. I didn't feel anything very much and that surprised me. It was all over. There was nothing left but the small change of living.

The past was dead and indestructible, so I told myself. Nothing could be altered now; perhaps in the beginning it could not have been altered because what had happened was the result of our weaknesses, our blind self-estimates, our pride, our false humilities. The end, though we could not have foreseen it, had been within us. It was small comfort and dishonest philosophy and as always I went back over the whole business, splitting and splintering the shape of the past, distorting it and twisting it and looking for the truth. And, as always, I went back to the beginning.

Nora and I had had a row before we went to the Hunters' party.

It was the usual sort of row about nothing in particular and it was conducted in the usual sort of way in savage, hushed whispers because the walls of our suburban house were thin and Nora's mother was in the next room. She had the radio on, but it was turned so low that she could not have been listening to it. She always did that, saying she did not want to wake the child, but it was really because she liked martyrdom. She also wanted to be able to hear what Nora and I said to each other so that she could persuade herself that I was a bad husband for her daughter. Not because she thought that I was a bad husband or even that Nora deserved someone better, but because she took pleasure in being a knowledgeable witness to unhappiness or failure. I knew, all the time we were angry with each other, that she was listening on the other side of the thin wall. I knew that she was sitting bolt upright in her chair with her interminable grey knitting on her lap, her fat knees spread out to the fire's heat, the glasses nodding on her nose and her mouth as tight as a trap. The knowledge was as bad as her presence would have been.

I think the row started because of Nora's dress. We had been quite friendly together before she put it on, after her bath. It was an old dress and not particularly becoming to her, and she knew it. She also knew that we couldn't afford another and therefore she wasn't able to make an issue of it. So we had a row about whether we should order a taxi to bring us home after the party or whether we should rely on someone giving us a lift back into the town. I have forgotten which of us wanted to order a taxi but it was not, even then, important.

We both said the same things that we always said on these occasions and the fact that the accusations were unoriginal and expected did not lessen their impact. They had sufficient truth in them to sting. Nora stood before the looking-glass, tugging at her dress. Her eyes shone with temper and her cheeks were flushed; she was normally too pale and the colour suited her. She said that life with me was intolerable, that if she had known it was going to be like this she would never have married me. It was the wail of a child worried and excited by the prospect of a party. She was almost thirty and social occasions still unnerved her.

I remember that I sat on the bed in my dinner-jacket and laced up my shoes and felt sad and ashamed because there was no reply to so many of the things she said. To be honest, I don't think she loved me as much as she always insisted, on these occasions, that she did; her love was just another stick to beat the dog with. Neither did she really believe that I was not still in love with her. We had had rows before when I had loved her with my whole heart and she had said much the same kind of thing with the same kind of hysterical bitterness. It had been easy to get angry with her then because I had been sure of loving her; it was impossible to get angry with her now. I began to feel the aching pain behind my eyes that was always there when we quarrelled. I got up from the bed and said that she was a silly goose and that it was stupid to quarrel, wasn't it, and spoil the evening?

In the end I made her laugh a little and she put lipstick on her mouth and combed her hair. We went together into Sandy's room. He looked a nice little urchin lying there asleep with his teddy bear across his chest and his collection of toy cars beside his head. I picked a small lorry off the pillow; the sharp edge of it had bruised the soft flesh below his eye. He stirred and smiled and sucked windily at the gap in his front teeth and Nora and I smiled across his sleeping head from sentimental habit. Convention decreed that this was the end of the row, the re-union by the bedside of the child, and until the taxi came we talked together with careful friendship.

It wasn't our kind of party. The Hunters weren't our kind of people and we weren't theirs, but we were asked, every year, to their duty cocktail party. This year I had not wanted to go, but Emily had said that it would look odd if we didn't come. And it wouldn't have been easy to explain to Nora. She didn't have much fun, poor child, although I think that she liked going out on this occasion not so much because she enjoyed herself when she got there as because being asked to the Hunters' party was a kind of assertion of status. We were professional people; the other people who lived in our street were not and they were not asked to the party. Most of them were better off than we were but I was the only man who owned a dinner-jacket. Nora would have been shocked if I had suggested that she was a snob.

She explained her attitude carefully.

"It isn't a matter of social standing, Tom. I haven't anything *in common* with them."

So during the three years we had lived in Sanctuary Road she had been sweet and remote with our working-class neighbours, holding high the shabby and pathetic banner of her university education. She liked to be seen carrying the new non-fiction books from the public library although she seldom finished them. She liked listening to the light programme and reading the popular women's magazines—I would find them carefully hidden under the sofa cushions—and she was ashamed of these things. Sometimes I was embarrassed for her and angry because of these small pretences. Now, thinking about them on the way to the Hunters' party, they made her seem vulnerable and sweet. I took her hand and held it and she leaned contentedly against me. I kissed her, not because I loved her, but because she was Nora who had been my wife for eight years and because, at this moment, I was glad that she was with me. She laced her fingers through mine and we sat in friendly silence like a happily married couple.

During the last decade the local rich had deserted the town's north suburb; the angular Victorian villas that had housed them were empty now of all but the oldest of the university fellows. The Hunters' village was fashionable and slightly phoney; their house fronted on to the main street. From the volume of noise that came from the open front door it sounded like a successful party.

Nora began to be nervous when she joined me in the hall after taking off her coat. She was holding one shoulder awkwardly and a little higher than the other in the way she had when she was unsure of herself. Her eyes were bright and panicky. I told her that she was looking lovely and good enough to eat; she grinned weakly and said that she felt like an early Christian being thrown to the lions, but that she would be all right once she'd had a drink.

The drawing-room smelt of gin and perfume and hothouse chrysanthemums. Clear middle-class voices cracked off the crystal of the chandeliers. We were late and sober and I badly needed a drink. There were rather too many waiters and rather too large and imposing a bar erected in front of the french windows. Emily's parties were always ostentatious. She wasn't showing off; it was the natural overflowing of a happily exuberant nature. She would have behaved in the same way, on a different scale, in a Glasgow slum.

I couldn't see her when we first went into the room, and I felt the absurd panic that I always felt when she was late for an appointment or didn't answer the telephone when I rang. I told myself that it was silly to feel like that and I made myself talk to Nora, find her a drink and light her cigarette. She was clinging and nervously chatty; I could never leave her at parties until she had drunk enough to be unself-conscious. I think that she was afraid I would leave her; she turned her back on the room and tried to entertain me with bright, strained gaiety as if I were not her husband and responsible for her.

I made her drink a double gin and then Geoffrey Hunter came to our rescue. He was a good host and he said all the right things. He told Nora that she looked charming and said how glad he was that we had been able to come. He was very emphatic about the gladness because we weren't the sort of people who usually came to his parties. I would have liked to think that he sounded insincere, but he didn't. He sounded gentle and assured and genuine, and I hated every inch of him from his flat, well-bred English face to his excellently-shod feet. He had no mannerisms, no tricks of speech. He didn't need them. He spoke softly and he had a scholar's face and amused, slightly prominent, blue eyes. But the confidence was there without the outward trappings; it came from some inner core of sureness that was quite unshakeable.

We talked for a little while and then he shepherded Nora away, shining and happy, to be introduced to some people whom, he said, he was sure she would like. He made it sound flattering as if he knew she would only like exceptional people.

Then I saw Emily and my heart lifted with delight. She was talking to a pair of middle-aged, wilting women who looked as if they might be the relics of country vicars. One of them had a dark growth of hair that sprouted from a mole on her chin and waggled as she talked. Emily seemed to be enjoying her party. I remember that I felt jealous because she could appear so happy when I was not there. She was wearing a long, tight dress made of green silk; the colour suited her and made her skin look pearly. I stood beside her and she turned and said:

"Tom, how nice. I'm so glad you could come."

Her voice was cool and social. She kept her hand on my arm while she introduced me to the grey women, and once she pinched me sharply through the stuff of my coat without any change of expression in her voice or on her face except for a quick, laughing look to see if I had winced. I hated meeting her at parties where there was no chance of our being alone together, but I think she got a certain amount of pleasure out of it as if we were children among the grown-ups, sharing a secret.

She said: "Mr. Harrington lectures at the university," and the two women looked admiring and said that it must be very interesting, such a pleasant job. It was clear that they thought I spent my days in a book-lined room with a decanter of port at my elbow and I longed to tell them that I lived in the sort of shabby, ill-built house that they barely knew existed. One of them was Lady Somebody or Other and the second one a plain Mrs., but I never sorted out which was which. They both wore the kind of shapeless dress that has a deep V-neck filled in with beige-coloured lace. We talked gardens and said how beautiful the dahlias were this year, perhaps it was a result of the wet summer? One of them had ordered her tulip bulbs from Holland. Bulbs, she said, made you realise that spring was not so very far away.

When we had exhausted the herbaceous border we smiled at each other with tight, determined smiles until Emily excused herself and said that she must go and see about the buffet supper.

She said, enjoying the game: "Perhaps you would be kind and help me, Tom?"

I was the willing guest. "I'd be delighted," I said.

We escaped to the damask-covered tables and counted knives and forks out of a varnished box. Her bare arm and shoulder were close to mine and her hair tickled my ear. I wanted to kiss her badly, and I suppose it was the effort of not doing so that blinded me to the fact that there was something wrong. Her face was flushed, her voice excited, and she was talking a great deal in a rather silly social way that was unlike her. I think I thought she had been drinking too much and too quickly.

Then she stopped talking and stared beyond me, over my shoulder. Her eyes frowned a little in the way they always did when she was worried or annoyed. She had lovely eyes, of an unexceptional and ordinary blue, but wide and bright and clear.

I turned round to see who she was looking at and saw Nora's brother David standing between two groups of people, quite alone, and watching us with sharp, attentive eyes. His stocky legs were placed wide apart, his chin thrust forward on to his big barrel of a chest. He seemed to find us amusing.

I said: "What's the matter? Shouldn't he be here?"

She didn't seem to have heard me, and so I repeated the question. She looked at me and said in a quick, confused way:

"Yes, of course he should. I mean, we sent an invitation to the paper. Geoffrey wants to keep in with the local press because of the election."

I said: "But you hoped he wouldn't be the one to come? It's all right. I don't go much of a bundle on my brother-in-law myself."

She grinned in an apologetic sort of way. "He hates Geoffrey," she said.

It was the one thing David and I agreed on, but I didn't say so. I suppose that in a way our dislike had the same kind of basis—the dislike of the half-failure for the man to whom failure is unthinkable. And in David's case it was more than that. He was a bitter Socialist and his politics were very personal affairs. He had expected to be the local Labour candidate and at the last minute he had been dropped for one of the public school brigade. We were a marginal seat and I imagined that the town's committee had wanted a bigger gun.

I said: "If he had his way he wouldn't give you much of a write-up for this. He's all against the fat man who waters the worker's beer. But he can't do Geoffrey any harm. He works for the wrong sort of paper."

She smiled, but not happily and then she bit her lip as if she were uneasy and alarmed about something, and I couldn't understand why. David was a nasty little trick, but he wasn't anyone to worry about. I wondered suddenly why she should be so sure that he hated Geoffrey. She might have known about the political business, but she couldn't have known how David would take it.

She said: "I think I'll go and talk to him."

She sounded abstracted. I said: "D'you have to? I should have thought not."

She said vaguely: "Duty talk, Tom. You ought to circulate, anyway. It's not very clever of us to stay together."

She left me and went to talk to David. They stood in a corner together; the hair curled on the nape of her neck as she bent her head towards him. She looked lovely; she was a tall, high-breasted girl with a wide Irish face, full of colour. Feature by feature she was not especially beautiful, her nose was too heavy and her mouth too full, but she had an air of almost extravagant health that made most women look drab beside her.

She was talking to David for a long time. I saw them from different points of the room while I talked inanities to a lot of people who were drinking more than was good for their stomachs or their souls. Emily was not smiling; she was listening to David with her head a little on one side and an intent, unhappy look on her face. There was an odd air of intimacy about them as they talked together which made me angry and hurt and jealous. Then she left him and the next time I saw her she was standing beside her husband. He was talking to the Vice-Chancellor and she stood with them for a while, smiling when she was spoken to, with a white, uncertain look. I had never seen her like that, without the life and the sparkle, and it made her look ten years older. After a short time she and Geoffrey went out of the room together.

I found David in the corner where Emily had left him. He was a little drunk and he grinned cheerfully at me. He was a fat, sweaty man who looked as if he never washed. He had the chest and shoulders of a heavyweight boxer and the remains of dashing good looks in his dark-eyed Welsh face. He had a thin, bitter mouth and there was something wrong with his teeth. At some point in his childhood he must have had two of his front side-teeth removed, bringing the sharp canines nearer to the front and giving him a vicious look. He was a provincial journalist and would never be anything else. He ran a gossip column and was excellently suited to the occupation; like his mother he delighted in malicious scandals and other people's failures. He was an infallible peddler of small nastiness.

He said: "Well, if it isn't Mr. High and Mighty Harrington. We're out of our class to-night, Tom, you and I."

I said: "You're having a good time, aren't you?"

He waved his drink at me. "Bloody capitalist's bloody booze," he said loudly and distinctly so that several people in our neighbourhood turned to look and smile. It was unexpected to find him drunk, he had a nonconformist attitude to drink which was odd in a journalist.

I said: "David, this is a polite party. Hadn't you better go home?"

He leered at me with his repulsive teeth like an evil pixie, and said: "You put on airs, Tom, with your dinner-jacket. Or are you sharing the social duties with our host? You have so much else in common."

The grin grew wider. His lips were damp and shining. I stood quite still, the sweat cold under my collar. He had seen us. At the time we hadn't been sure. We had come out of my room in college, careless with happiness; it must have been written on our faces. David, who occasionally ran an article on university doings, had been in the quadrangle talking to an undergraduate. I had seen him and pulled Emily back into the archway. It had been a silly thing, a guilty thing to do, and almost at once we had walked straight out into the quadrangle and smiled at him in greeting. I had hoped that he had not seen my instinctive, revealing movement and afterwards I had forgotten about the whole thing. But of course he had noticed, of course he knew.

I said: "You're a swine, aren't you?" trying to sound confident and angry. He went on grinning at me in a sly and stupid way so that I wanted to hit him.

He was too drunk to be careful. He said: "You mustn't think you are specially honoured, Tom. The lady isn't particular."

That went too near the bone. I didn't care who heard me. I said: "Get out, you bastard, or I'll throw you out."

He laughed, throwing back his big head, the oiled hair shedding white scurf on to his collar. A number of people near us stopped talking and stared openly. Then Geoffrey joined us. He was taller than most of the men in the room; his pale face was politely smiling. The fair hair on his cheekbones glinted in the light.

He said: "Mr. Parry, I've been looking for you. Would you come and have a drink with me in the library?"

It was the voice of confident authority; it sank through the layers of resentment and inverted snobbery. David looked defiant, but he said, quite submissively: "Yes, I don't mind if I do, Mr. Hunter."

They went off together. Geoffrey, for his height and sex, extraordinarily graceful and the little fat horror waddling beside him like a goose. Geoffrey held the door open for him and he ducked through it awkwardly and without dignity, his tight jacket rucked up over his fat behind.

Emily was beside me. She looked quiet and pale, and the mascara was smudged at the corners of her eyes as though she had been crying. She said: "Thank God for that."

I felt churlish. "He's got the lordly manner all right, hasn't he?"

She gave me a quick, wan smile. "Tom, don't be bitter. You don't have to be jealous of Geoffrey."

I wondered suddenly how many men she had said that to. I said: "All right. But the lord of the manor act makes me feel plebeian. Besides, he's at least four inches taller than I am. What were you talking to Parry about?"

She said, and she was always a bad liar: "Nothing, Tom. Local scandal. He is really rather amusing when he chooses to be."

"He knows about us. Was that what he was telling you?"

"No, Tom. I've told you what we talked about. And I don't expect he knows about us either. No more than a lucky guess, anyway. He's too wily to act on guesswork."

I was at first surprised that she could be so confident and appear to mind so little, and then I felt the familiar bitterness of wondering how often this had happened to her before that she could treat it so lightly. She out her hand on my arm, and said:

"Quite a lot of people have gone. Do you think the others would like to dance?"

The polished floor was bare and we had nothing to do except choose the records for the radiogram. I suppose, looking back, that we behaved foolishly and conspicuously, but I was more than a little drunk and Emily seemed to want me to be with her. We put on a record that we both knew and liked and started the dancing. Emily danced beautifully; she was tall for a woman and I was short for a man so that our steps fitted comfortably together. I liked dancing with her and after a little she leaned against me as if she were tired. She didn't talk very much, and I suppose I should have known then that something was troubling her, but I was still thinking about David and hoping Nora had not seen what had happened.

After we had danced for about half an hour, I saw Nora. She was with the senior lecturer in music and his dull wife. She was leaning against the wall with a drink in one hand and a cigarette in the other. I smiled at her over Emily's shoulder, and she grinned bravely. I felt worried about her and when the record ended and we walked over to the gramophone to choose another I said that I thought I ought to go and dance with her.

Emily said: "Oh, Tom, must you?" And, for a moment, because she looked tired and not well I had the same grinding feeling of responsibility for her that I always had for Nora. But she said, before I could answer: "How silly of me. Of course you must go and dance with her, Tom." She turned away, dismissing me, and walked over to the buffet tables.

I rescued Nora from the music lecturer. We danced a slow waltz rather badly and out of step with each other. She was a little drunk and fondled my neck with one hand.

I said: "Are you enjoying the party?" and she shook her head.

"Not much. It's too noisy and all the people are dull." I must have sighed because she immediately looked anxious and said brightly: "I suppose I'm just out of the social habit. I haven't read the new books, or seen the new plays."

It was the usual, indirect complaint, and I said defensively: "This isn't a literary society, you know." After that we didn't talk at all and when the waltz ended I took her along to the bank manager and his wife. He was a purple-faced, merry man and could be relied upon to be nice to everyone, including Nora.

After that the evening became a little blurred. I danced with Emily almost continuously. The crowd had thinned and I knew, distantly, that we would be discussed over coffee in the morning. Emily was usually clever about that sort of thing, but to-night she didn't seem to care. She didn't talk much and she didn't always answer when I spoke to her. Her silence didn't worry me. I was happy to be with her; we had been lovers for almost a year and I found her, still, a constant and surprising joy.

At about eleven o'clock Nora came up to us as we sat at a table, eating sandwiches. She said:

"Tom, I'm sorry. It's a headache."

She looked nervous and contrite. Her mouth was screwed up and her face was white with pain. She often had a headache when she was not enjoying herself. The pain was quite real and sometimes almost blinded her, but it didn't always help to know that.

Emily said: "I'm so sorry. Would an aspirin do any good? We were thinking of going to the golf club when the party ended and we had hoped you would be able to come."

Nora said: "No. Tom, take me home." She sounded like a rude child and her eyes filled with tears so that for a moment I was almost angry with Emily for being unpercipient, forgetting that I had told her about Nora's headaches and their usual cause. Nora turned her back on us and went to the door.

I said: "Emily, I'm sorry." And she smiled at me with her wide mouth and lovely eyes, and said:

"It's a shame. Poor Tom."

Her sympathy and the feeling of conspiracy between us made me feel a traitor. I thought of Nora with uneasy guilt; the knowledge that I didn't love her made me see her as perhaps more pathetic than she really was. I said good-bye to Emily and followed Nora to the door.

She had gone upstairs to get her coat and I waited in the empty hall with the noise of the gramophone coming through the open door. It was cold in the hall and I wished that I had brought my coat with me.

The library door opened and David came out. He stood in the doorway, and said over his shoulder:

"Mr. Hunter, has nothing ever come between you and the sun?"

It was a consciously dramatic exit line and, as such, coming from the drunken Welshman, should have sounded absurd, but for some reason it did not. There was so much resentment in his voice and bitter anger that the effect of his words was chilling.

Geoffrey Hunter said something from inside the room, but I could not hear what it was. David shrugged his heavy shoulders and turned away, walking through the hall with the cautious solemnity of the drunk. Geoffrey followed him. He didn't see me and his face was drawn with temper.

He said: "You'll keep your mouth shut, you little runt, d'you hear?"

Then he saw me and his face composed miraculously into civilised restraint. At least the features were composed, the eyes were cold as charity. David passed me, staring straight ahead, and went into the street through the open door.

Geoffrey looked at me. His back was to the light and I couldn't see his face very clearly. He said:

"He's a bore, that man. I didn't think he'd come." His voice was deliberately light, rather strained. I wondered whether David had told him about Emily and me, but it was impossible to tell.

Nora and I went home in the back of the bank manager's car. She lay with her head on my shoulder and moaned gently every now and again. By the time they brought us to our gate she was almost asleep. I helped her out of the car and she stood beside me, swaying a little, while I said good night and thanked them for the ride.

When we got indoors she went straight upstairs and I made her a warm drink and took it up to her. She was sitting in bed; she had washed the make-up from her face, leaving traces of lipstick in small gobs at the corner of her mouth.

She said: "Tom, why do you leave me alone so much?"

I put the tray carefully on the bedside table.

I said slowly: "My dear, I thought you liked to go out to meet other people, not to be with me."

She said accusingly: "You know that isn't true. You know that I love you and like you to be with me."

She started to cry helplessly and drunkenly, the tears rolled out of the corners of her eyes and splashed on to the sheets. She looked sweet and plain and rather young. We were off again and there wasn't anything that I could do to stop it. The old angers and resentments came out with hideous inevitability. I said nothing and I looked at her—at the small, pale face and the cloud of dark hair and the mouth spoiled with temper. It was my face. I had lived with it and made it and I couldn't escape the responsibility.

She had thought I was someone quite different when she had married me. I don't think I had been; if I had encouraged her to think I was a different sort of person it was only because I had tried to tell her about the sort of person that I had wanted to be. Her accusations weren't really levelled at me, but at the man I had hoped, in my early twenties, to become. I had never really been in love with her although I had persuaded myself that I was. She had been someone I had thought I could mould into my idea of what my wife should be. I knew now that it was a wrong thing to have done and a cruel thing, and I was bitterly ashamed.

14

In the end she said: "Tom, you do love me, don't you?"

I said: "Of course, silly goose. It's too late to quarrel. Be a good girl now, and go to sleep."

I opened the curtains and turned out the lights and got into bed.

She said, in the dark: "Tom, I was so ashamed about David."

Her voice was muffled and far more intensely miserable than when she had been quarrelling with me. Shame was always, for her, a more potent cause of unhappiness than anger.

I lied. "I don't think many people noticed him. And, anyway, it doesn't reflect on you."

She didn't answer and the bed shook a little as if she were crying to herself. We lay with our backs to each other in the awful intimacy of the double bed, not touching each other until sleep was too imminent to prevent it and then we lay closer, warmly curled and in some measure comforted.

Chapter Two

The telephone woke me. The room was washed with the dead, grey light of an early morning without sun. I got out of bed, yawning and muzzy with sleep, and brushed my hair before the looking-glass. I always brushed my hair as soon as I got up, even if I was in a hurry, and it was something that never failed to irritate Nora so that now I glanced instinctively at her sleeping, tumbled body to see if she were awake and watching me.

The telephone was in the sitting-room by the window. The curtains were open and outside it was a wet, muggy morning. The drab line of houses opposite looked as unreal as houses in a stage set, their windows empty and dead and cold. The mist steamed in the street.

Emily said: "Tom, is that you? Darling, there's been some trouble. Can I see you?"

The carpet was rough under my bare feet. There was a badly frayed patch by the telephone table, and I could feel the wooden floor beneath. I was very cold.

I said: "What's the matter?" It was a foolish thing to say because I knew what was the matter. Emily had never rung me up at home before.

She said: "Geoffrey knows about us. I think you were right about your brother-in-law. I think he must have said something to Geoffrey. He asked me and I told him."

I said: "Oh, God!" And then: "How frightful for you. What's happened?"

She sounded very dead. "I'm not sure. Geoffrey's being very civilised."

I said: "Do you want me to see him?"

She hesitated. "I don't know. But I'd like you to come. Would you mind?"

Her voice sounded unsure and a little scared as if she didn't know how I was going to take it. Almost as though she were afraid of me.

I said: "Darling, of course I'll come. Straight away." And I added, stupidly: "Try not to worry."

"No," she said. "Bless you." And the line went dead.

In moments of utter disaster you don't really think or feel anything exceptional or unexpected. Your actions are not so much your own as the automatic responses learned from stage and screen as being the inevitable expression of catastrophe. You light a cigarette from the packet on the mantelpiece and stub it out again almost immediately. You look round for a drink, not because you want one, but because it seems the conventional thing to do. Then the sensation of theatre fades the sweat dries on your forehead and the quick pulse slows down. The individual questions stick out like thumb marks on a clean wall. Why in God's name did it have to happen? Did the telephone wake Nora? What am I to say to her? Is there a puncture in my bicycle tyre? What am I going to do?

I pulled my pyjama jacket tighter round my chest and tucked it into my trousers. I went slowly upstairs, carefully avoiding the stair that creaked when you trod on it.

Nora was still asleep. She turned over and sighed as I went into the room, but her eyes were closed. I remember that I felt an absurd sense of relief because I would not have to explain why I was dressing myself at this early hour. I collected my clothes and took them to the bathroom. I washed and dressed as quickly as I could and wondered if I ought to shave and decided against it. I went down the stairs, my shoes in my hand. I was sitting on the bottom stair and putting them on when Nora said:

"Tom, what on earth are you doing? Has the clock stopped?"

She was standing on the landing, leaning over the banisters. Her dark hair fell about her face and her shoulders were white above her nightdress. She always looked very pretty in the mornings before the day began to cloud her face with worry. Her smile was puzzled and sweet.

I said: "I didn't mean to wake you up. I couldn't sleep. I thought I'd go out for a bit."

I was always surprised how easy it was to lie. The thing that hurt was the trustful acceptance and belief.

She said: "But, Tom, it's so early and so cold. Must you?"

I said: "Dear, go back to bed. I'll come home soon and make breakfast."

She said reluctantly: "All right," and I went upstairs and tucked her up in bed. The pulse in my throat was beating so hard I was afraid she would notice it. But she didn't. She smiled at me sleepily and I kissed her because she seemed to expect it. I felt like Judas.

The tyres of my bicycle were flat and I pumped them up angrily. I cycled as fast as I could; the raw, damp mist was unpleasant to breathe and made me cough. My hands were sticky on the handlebars and I thought that it was a long time since I had sweated with fear.

I cycled out of the town, sleeping and empty in the early morning, and along the road to the village. The mist cleared a little as the road climbed out of the valley. It was autumn and going to be a berry winter; the hedges were already black and bare. In the fields beyond the hedges they had started the ploughing and in the distance the wooded hills were dim and blue. When I was a child we had lived in a cottage on the farm where my father had been cowman. I had cycled to the grammar school in the town on so many mornings like this one that now I felt a sudden, sentimental regret for a time when life had been full of possibilities and there was no thought of failure. It had been like that, or almost like that, until I had got the university lectureship I had coveted for so long and then life had become ordinary and dull and everyday. I had reached out for the star and there was nothing in my hand but dust. I felt a surge of immense compassion for the boy who had thought the world lay at his feet and had grown to discover that it lay instead at the feet of people like Geoffrey Hunter.

I was only escaping from the reality of the moment and perhaps not even that. Because what was happening now, and what had happened when Emily spoke to me on the telephone, did not seem to be real at all.

At the beginning of the village I passed a boy on a Fordson tractor, bumping uncomfortably in his slow-moving seat. He was about fourteen; as I passed him on my bicycle he called "Good morning," and grinned at me with embarrassed pride and a swagger of his shoulders.

The main street of the village was quiet; the Georgian houses, tranquil and asleep. I propped my bicycle against the kerb, took off my trouser clips and rang the bell of Emily's house. I wished suddenly that I had been able to come in a car; the bicycle made me feel like an errand boy.

Emily came to the door. She was wearing a woollen dressing-gown which was too big for her and her face was tired and looked rubbed out at the edges. She smiled at me stiffly.

She said: "Tom, it was wonderful of you to come. I've made some coffee."

We went into the little morning-room at the front of the house. There was a freshly-stoked fire and the room was littered with crates of empty bottles and ash trays that had not been cleared after the party. The air smelt frowsty and the cold daylight was pitiless to Emily's white face. She stretched out her hands to the fire and the fingers were cramped and bloodless at the knuckles. She looked unhappy; I wanted to comfort and reassure her, but I could think of nothing to say. I kissed her and she held me tightly for a moment. Then she said, with embarrassed formality:

"You must be frozen, Tom. Sit down and I'll give you some coffee."

She fussed with the coffee tray like a shy hostess after a heavy-footed dinner-party. Her hands were shaking and when she gave me my cup she smiled brightly and uneasily as if I were a stranger she was afraid to talk to.

I gulped at my coffee and it scalded my throat. I said: "You'd better tell me what happened." I felt a million miles away from her.

She looked all of her thirty-five years; she turned her back on me and walked to a chair by the window, feeling slowly for the arm before she sat down, like an old woman.

She sat facing me, her hands folded, in her lap. She said: "Tom, I can't tell you how sorry I am. I would never have told him. Only I thought he knew."

"Didn't he?"

"I'm not sure, now. I thought he did know. It wasn't until afterwards that I thought it might be just a guess. I think David *did* say something to him—but nothing sure. It was because Geoffrey was acting so oddly that I thought he must know."

She twisted the dressing-gown cord tightly round and round her fingers and then jerked it away, leaving white marks across the back of her hand.

They hadn't gone to the golf club. The party had died soon after we had left. Emily had seen the last of the guests into their car and gone upstairs to have a bath. There had been no sign of Geoffrey but she had not been particularly disturbed, assuming that he had gone into the study to work.

He had come into the bedroom when she had finished her bath and was sitting at the dressing-table, brushing her hair. She saw him, in the looking-glass, standing by the door. Her first thought was that he was ill; she had never seen him so white. She asked him if he was sick and he didn't seem to hear her. She was suddenly and inexplicably afraid, she got up from the dressing-stool and crossed the room. She touched his arm and he started violently as though he had not noticed she was in the room. He stared at her as if she were a stranger.

He said: "How the hell did Parry find out?"

Emily said: "For a moment I couldn't think what he was talking about. Then I remembered what you had said. So I told him, without thinking, that I supposed David had seen us together. His expression changed then—before, he'd looked angry and now, quite suddenly, he looked just curious. He said: 'So it was true about you and Harrington?' I told him yes, that it was true. I think that

I was still a little drunk. I said that I loved you and that I wasn't sorry."

She flushed defiantly, and said: "Was it stupid to say that?"

I said: "No, not stupid. Just adorable." But it couldn't have sounded very convincing and there was disappointment on her face. I said quickly: "What happened then?"

She sounded weary, a little as if the fight had gone out of her.

There had been a row and it had gone on and on interminably. They had talked, she said, in cliches. Everything that had been said was a platitude from a third-class romantic novel. In the beginning she had been exalted, almost happy because there was no more hypocrisy or deceit; it was a relief to be able to say that she was proud and pleased to love me. Then the reaction had set in. And the inevitable sentimentality.

She said: "I hadn't thought about Geoffrey for a long time. Not as a person. He was my husband and I was concerned for him and fond of him. And suddenly I began to see him more clearly, as if he were not my husband but an ordinary, pathetic human being. I was sorry for him. Not because he loves me or because he needs me, but because he is so vulnerable where his pride is concerned. Of course I'd known the scandal would worry him because of the election, but I hadn't really thought it would matter so very much. It was just one of Geoffrey's dreams of grandeur. It wasn't until we had been talking for about two hours that I knew just how important it was to him. These things matter so much more to him than to other people. The idea that he might lose his seat meant that the whole world had crumpled beneath him. Do you understand, Tom?"

She looked at me with a white, baffled face. I wanted to comfort her, to tell her that it wasn't the most important thing in the world that something should go wrong for Geoffrey when most things, up to now, had gone right for him. That he was not a pathetic figure just because he was so much more sure than other people that he ought to succeed in everything that he had tried to do. But at that moment there was something much more important to say.

I said it. "Darling, what do you want me to do?"

She looked at me with wonder as if she could not understand my question. She said: "Please, Tom, take me away."

I suppose it was something that I had been expecting and dreading ever since the telephone call. Of course, to her, it would seem to be the only outcome and I had known, always, that if we were ever found out it was what she would expect me to do. But for the last hour I had shut my mind against the knowledge. Perhaps I had been hoping for a miracle.

I didn't look at her. I said: "Darling, I can't. You know I can't."

She didn't say anything and I stumbled on in a kind of panic, knowing that the things I was saying were sensible enough, but that they must sound, to Emily, like the shabby reasoning of fear. I said that Nora trusted me, that she depended on me and that there was the child. That it was unthinkable that I should ever leave her; that I couldn't support her if I did and that I was responsible for her. And that, to Nora, if I left her, the thing that would hurt her most would be the shame of the neighbours' gossiping. I was suddenly immensely moved by a wave of protective affection for her; I thought of her with guilt and pity and a kind of love.

When I had finished I knew that Emily had not understood at all. She said, in a shocked voice: "But do you love her. Tom?"

I said: "Darling, not in the way that I love you. But that isn't the whole of it, is it?"

She got up from her chair, stumbling awkwardly over her long dressing-gown and looked in the box for a cigarette. The box was empty and I found a squashed packet in my trouser pocket and lit one for her. The small movements helped us both over the embarrassment of the moment. Then she said:

"Poor, poor Tom. What a hideous, awful mess for you." She tried to smile at me, and I felt a swine.

I said helplessly: "Emily, do you hate me?"

She shook her head and this time she smiled without any effort. "Of course not," she said. "Why should I hate you?"

She crouched on the sofa beside me and stroked my face. I took her hand and held it.

Geoffrey said, from the door: "Good morning, Tom."

I dropped Emily's hand as if it were red-hot and then felt ashamed and would have taken it again. But she got up swiftly from the sofa and moved to the fireplace where she stood, turned away from both of us, warming her hands before the fire.

The skin of his face was smooth and pink from shaving. He was wearing an old Etonian tie and an expensively shabby sports coat. His flaxen hair was sleekly brushed, he was an English gentleman dressed for a day in the country. He looked calm, rested and slightly amused. I got up from the sofa because I didn't like him looking down at me any more than his natural advantage in height made inevitable.

He looked at Emily. He said: "Dear, is there any coffee left?"

There was a silence while Emily poured out a cup of coffee and Geoffrey settled himself comfortably in a chair and lit a pipe with what appeared to be genuine composure. I did not look at Emily. I felt wretchedly like a small boy on the mat in the headmaster's study. The silence went on and on.

At last Geoffrey looked up from his coffee. He said: "Well, Tom, you've got yourself into a charming little scrape, haven't you?"

His voice was soft and tolerant and almost kind. It put me more in the wrong than any display of anger would have done. There was no possible answer. For a moment Geoffrey waited politely for me to speak and then he said:

"Emily tells me you love her. Do you?"

I loved her more than I had ever loved anyone or anything in my whole life, but it was impossible to say so at this moment and to this man.

I tried. I said: "I love her very much." It sounded stiff and inadequate and remarkably false.

He examined the bowl of his pipe as if he were unwilling to watch me make a fool of myself.

"Of course if you love her, it makes it all the more serious," he said. "It's gone on for some time, I believe."

"Almost a year," I said.

He looked at me with sandy-lashed, light eyes. "I see." He spoke with the slow deliberation of a judge. I remember that all the time he was speaking I looked at his hands, at the long, beautiful fingers holding the coffee-cup and the pipe.

"Of course," he said, "I'm not disputing your love for my wife. That would be presumptuous of me. But I have been married to Emily for eleven years. This isn't the first time that I've had to get her out of a scrape of this kind. So you must forgive me if I am a little cynical about her attitude towards you. It is not that she is promiscuous, you understand, merely that she has a very affectionate if undiscriminating nature."

Emily was sitting hunched up on a hassock in front of the fire, her head turned away from me, and he smiled in her direction like a kindly uncle smiling at a wayward but well-meaning child.

"You must realise," he said, "that while you have been in love with my wife you haven't had any responsibility for her. I imagine, therefore, that quite a lot of your pleasure has been at my expense. Do you really think, Tom, that if I were willing to divorce her, you could make her happier than I have done? After all, I am not only a comparatively rich but also a complaisant husband."

His smile held all the confidence in the world. I felt no guilt at all, only impotent anger. I would have liked to hit him and I suspect, from the amusement in his eyes, that he knew how I felt.

He waited. Then he looked at Emily's averted head. "Perhaps I am misreading the situation? Perhaps you don't want to marry her?"

Emily said, before I could speak: "Tom can't leave his wife." She did not turn her head and in the droop of her shoulders and the dead tone of her voice there was pathetic and complete acceptance and submission.

"Nora knows nothing about it," I said.

He made a monosyllabic, judicial sound in the back of his throat.

"I am glad," he said, "that you have some notion of responsibility. Emily has none. I tried to explain to her what your attitude would be but once she gets an idea in her head she is not very amenable to advice."

Emily began to cry in a quiet, choked way. I had never seen her cry before and I stood, like a fool, and watched her. Geoffrey did not move. He lay back in his chair looking at her speculatively and without pity. When I could bear it no longer I went over to her and put my hand lightly on her shoulder. She twisted round on the hassock and leaned her head against my thigh.

Geoffrey said heavily: "Harrington, I don't think this is in very good taste in the circumstances, do you?"

It was intentional unkindness posing as anger. Emily got up as if he had struck her. Her face was burning.

She said: "Geoffrey, I didn't think it was possible to dislike anyone so much. Tom, I am terribly sorry to have dragged you into this."

She crossed the room and sat by the window, staring out into the street that was washed, now, by a pale and showery sun. The mist had gone and there was a nursery-blue sky with puffs of cotton-wool cloud.

Geoffrey looked at Emily and then he gave me a wry, man-to-man smile. He said: "I suppose I should apologise for my last remark. But you must allow me some atavistic feelings."

I had never felt so helpless. I think that I tried to stammer out some kind of apology and vindication, but it sounded pretty weak and unconvincing and Geoffrey listened to me with one eyebrow raised.

In the end, he said: "How are you going to explain all this to your wife?"

It was like a blow in the stomach. I said: "I hadn't thought—is there any need for her to know?"

Geoffrey looked surprised. "No, I suppose there isn't any need. It would be gratuitous cruelty."

He waited for a moment as if he were expecting me to say something and then he said: "She'll be wondering what has happened to you, won't she?" He got out of his chair. "I'll wait for you in the hall," he said.

He went out of the room and closed the door carefully behind him. Emily turned from the window and held out her arms. Her face was wet as she kissed me.

"Darling," she said, "I didn't think he'd behave like this. It was horrible for you." Her concern was completely genuine, she was untouched by any kind of humiliation or resentment.

I said: "Emily, I'm sorry. I'm sorry." There was nothing else I could say. We were both whispering like punished children.

I said: "He didn't seem to me like a man who was very deeply disturbed."

She looked bewildered. "I don't understand, Tom," she said. "Perhaps it was just an act. He's very proud—he wouldn't let you know that he was upset, would he?"

I didn't think that Geoffrey had been putting on an act. He had been enjoying himself too much. But there was no point in saying so.

She clung to me, her fingers digging painfully into my upper arm. "Tom," she said. "don't stop seeing me, will you? I couldn't bear it, it would be impossible."

I had never seen Emily as a suppliant before and it disturbed me. Perhaps if I had said then that we must make an end of it it might all have worked out differently. But I hadn't the courage. Just then I would have needed courage, not because I loved her, but because she needed me.

I said: "Darling, of course we'll see each other somehow. Don't worry."

I kissed her and then she said: "Go along now, Tom. I'll write to you."

Geoffrey was standing in the hall by the open front door, looking appreciatively at the sky.

"Looks as if it is going to be a decent day," he said.

I went out on to the pavement and he followed me, standing beside me while I put on my trouser clips. My front tyre was flat again and I pumped it up.

Then he said: "You know, Tom, I'm really very sorry for you. But these things happen to the best of us from time to time. You mustn't feel too much of a bastard."

I am quite sure that he did not mean to patronise. It was just that he was so very sure of himself and so safe.

He said: "I think, for all our sakes, that it would be better if you didn't see Emily again. Oh, I don't mean that you should avoid each other, that would be absurd and it's not necessary anyway, but you should not make any further arrangements to meet. After all, this is a small town and the society we live in is even smaller. It wouldn't do you any good in your job if there were any scandal and university appointments aren't easy to come by."

I wondered if it was advice or a threat. I was an undistinguished lecturer and lecturers are easily replaced. Geoffrey had a finger in most local pies and the Vice-Chancellor was a friend of his.

My mouth was dry. "I am not prepared to promise anything," I said.

He grinned in a cold and angry way. "I think you'll have to make up your mind," he said.

"You think you win all along the line, don't you?"

He said: "Come now, Tom. We've been fairly amicable so far, haven't we? You're getting off pretty lightly, you know."

I got on my bicycle and rode off down the street, conscious that it was an undignified kind of departure. He called after me as if this were an ordinary, social parting: "Give my love to Nora, Tom."

I remember that as I rode back to the town I felt a primitive and raging hatred that I had never felt before. I was physically sick with it; I got off my bicycle and vomited in a ditch. I had never felt before that I wanted to kill a man.

Nora was in the kitchen, making breakfast. The hair fell over her forehead and her cheek was smudged. She was wearing the down-at-heel slippers that she kept for working in the house and the vein that marked the back of her bare leg looked blue and swollen and sore.

She said: "Where have you been, Tom? It's so thoughtless . . ."

I said: "I'm sorry. I didn't mean to be late. Can I help?"

She went on: "Mother had a bad night and wants her breakfast in bed. And we're late already."

Then she made an obvious effort, and said: "I don't mean to be cross. I've got a terrible hangover."

I felt, suddenly, perhaps because of guilt or insecurity, that she had never seemed so dear. Because she looked plain and tired and harassed she seemed to be infinitely precious. I wanted to kiss her and promise to look after her, to reassure both of us. And I was appalled at myself and my own hypocrisy.

I laid breakfast and helped Sandy to get ready for school. He was quarrelsome and difficult at breakfast, and Nora looked more and more miserably worried until he finally departed, slamming the door behind him.

I helped Nora to wash up the dishes and then I bathed and shaved and changed my clothes. I had a lecture at ten o'clock but I felt a curious reluctance to leave the house. I followed Nora from room to room, not wanting to talk to her, but wanting to be with her, until in the end she said pettishly: "For heaven's sake, Tom, you'll be late, won't you?"

She put up her cheek to be kissed and her hair brushed my cheek. It was soft and smelt of bacon fat. I collected my books and lecture notes and left the house as if it were an ordinary morning.

Chapter Three

There was a note from Emily waiting for me when I got to my room after the lecture. It said she would be in the bar of the Woolpack before lunch and would I meet her there? She sent her love and three scrawled kisses at the bottom of the page.

The Woolpack was the town's main hotel. It was darkly and expensively Tudor, and the bar was always crowded and noisy so that it was, in effect, a very private place to meet.

I had a tutorial at twelve o'clock with a slow and spotty youngster who worked heartbreakingly hard and would be lucky if he got a pass degree. I cut him short by about twenty minutes and then felt guilty about it when I saw the hurt surprise on his face.

Emily was sitting at a table at the end of the long bar with a gin and tonic in front of her. The sun came in through the window behind her and gilded her hair. She looked lovely in a peaches and cream way as if she had slept for a long, untroubled night. The tweeds she was wearing were new and suited her. Two men standing at the bar were gaping at her with open admiration.

I had been prepared to find her unhappy and worn; I should have remembered that she was more resilient than anyone I had ever known. I sat down opposite her and she smiled at me with love and pleasure as if there was nothing wrong at all.

I said: "You look a honey. Like an Ovaltine advertisement. Or a *Vogue* model wearing the right clothes on a Scottish moor."

She said: "Dearest Tom, I love you." As if that was the only thing that mattered. It would have been pleasant, because she looked so lovely and the sun was shining, to have fostered the illusion.

I said: "Does Geoffrey know you have come to see me?"

She frowned. "I don't know. I think he does. He thought he would be able to scare you into not seeing me. I'm so very glad he couldn't do that."

She stretched her hand across the table. Her rings cut into the fleshy part of my fingers.

I said, uncomfortably: "It isn't going to be easy now he knows about it. He's not likely to accept the situation, is he?"

"What can he do?" She sounded puzzled, not apprehensive.

"He could make himself unpleasant, couldn't he?" And I glanced instinctively over my shoulder as if I had expected to see him standing there.

I saw David. He was standing with his back to us and talking to a group of undergraduates, five or six young men who laughed loudly and dutifully every now and again. I had always, when I wasn't disliking him, been sorry for David because he needed an audience so badly. And because it was only the first year undergraduates who collected about him, scandalised and impressed by his malicious, clever tongue. After a term or so they drifted away, bored or embarrassed, and I suspected that they laughed at him behind his back. He was wearing a filthy raincoat and the bottoms of his trouser legs were impressed and muddy. I hoped he hadn't seen us.

Emily said: "Geoffrey never goes to pubs," and she smiled at me in the amused and private way she had when she knew what I was thinking about without my telling her.

Then she said: "Are you really worried, Tom? He's not likely to do anything about it, even if he could. It's only an open scandal that he minds about."

I said, and I think I was a little angry that she should be so secure and safe in her belief that Geoffrey could do nothing:

"Do you really think it is as simple as that? That we can go on seeing each other? That I need not tell Nora if we do?"

She said: "Was it ever simple, Tom? And is it worse to deceive Nora now that Geoffrey knows, than it was before?"

I said: "Of course it is worse," and felt a fool.

Then I tried to explain, both to Emily and to myself, why this should be so, and it sounded illogical and merely silly. I said that she was right in thinking that the moral issues involved were unchanged, that Geoffrey's knowledge had merely presented them afresh. That what I was feeling now was nothing new but only the same appalled feeling of guilt that I had felt in the beginning and grown used to through the months so that until now I had ceased to feel it either deeply or sharply.

She grinned in the way she always grinned when I was being pompous.

She said: "Darling, it isn't only that. While no one knew about it we were able to persuade ourselves that it wasn't an ordinary, shabby affair. The sort of thing you read about in the Sunday newspapers. Now Geoffrey knows about it, it isn't so easy to feel like that. You touch the bright bubble and all you have is a watery mess."

She blushed brightly and looked immediately shy, as if she had not intended to say anything so dramatic and give herself away so completely. We had never pretended that our affair was justified because we loved each other; it would have sounded too much like special pleading. And I had been too wary of my own motives to say that my love for her was something different and set apart. I think, too, that I had been afraid she would think me naïve and laugh at me. I remember that I was suddenly quite astonishingly grateful because Emily appeared to feel, in a way I had not expected, that our relationship was more important than we had ever allowed ourselves to admit. We looked at each other with the embarrassment of people confronted with an emotion that had always been understated and treated, for the most part, lightly.

I said, self-consciously: "I expect I've just been badly scared."

And then I went to buy her another drink. While I was standing at the bar, David turned and saw me. He nodded and raised his glass. He was drinking tomato juice. I waited for him to start talking to his young men before I took our drinks back to the table.

When I sat down, Emily said: "Tom, would you rather not see me again?"

It wasn't the prelude to an outburst of feminine reproaches; she really wanted to know. When I said nothing, she went on anxiously:

"You know, I would understand that it wasn't because you didn't love me."

She couldn't have made it easier for me. I knew then that if I were to say it was what I wanted, she would have accepted it without resentment, not because she understood, but because she loved me.

"Of course I want to see you," I said, and when she smiled it was like the sun coming out. I felt ashamed because of my own small and completely conscious desire to have done with the whole thing.

She said: "Tom, you mustn't dislike Geoffrey too much. He doesn't mean to talk like a pompous ass. I think he honestly tries to be fair and to see our side of it. After you'd gone this morning he was upset because he said he had felt like a schoolmaster, and he was afraid you had resented him."

I said: "It's Geoffrey's great art. Decent chapmanship. Something Stephen Potter forgot about. Puts everyone else in the wrong."

She giggled. "I love you, Tom."

I said crossly: "Oh, you're quite right. He behaved beautifully this morning. He didn't attack me with a hatchet and he hadn't beaten you—or had he? All I know is that the next time I want a mistress I'll get myself the wife of a simple, hot-headed dock labourer. It would be far less humiliating to have one's head split open, don't you think?"

Emily said: "Oh, for God's sake, Tom." Then: "I'm sorry. Poor darling. It was abominably unpleasant. I know how you felt. But it was the situation, not Geoffrey."

I said: "And my own over-developed sense of class inferiority."

She said: "Tom, don't be silly," in a bewildered and slightly irritated way. It was something about me that she had never understood and would never understand. I think she thought it was just a joke, in rather bad taste.

I remembered something that had bothered me. I said: "Why did David tell Geoffrey about us? At the party you said that he hated Geoffrey. Why did you say that?"

She looked at me with troubled eyes. There were bracken-coloured flecks in the blue colour round the pupil.

She said: "Do you really want to know?"

I nodded and she shifted uneasily in her seat and fiddled with the metal clasp of her handbag. She lit a cigarette nervously and then she told me about it. It was a simple and nasty little story and I wondered why she had bothered to be so elusive about it.

When they had first moved to the town—about a year before I had known them—they had met David at a party. I gathered that it was the sort of party they would not go to now and that they had only accepted the invitation because they were strangers in the town. David had been in one of his brighter moods and they had found him amusing. He could be very witty when he chose and before you came to the end of his funny stories. For a while they had seen him fairly frequently, at least Emily said that she had seen him. She was vague about how the friendship had developed, perhaps intentionally, perhaps because it had really been unimportant to her. It was impossible to tell. She said that in the end she began to meet him accidentally in the town and that the meetings had been curiously frequent as if he had contrived them. One day she had had lunch with him, and David had asked her to go to bed with him. He had seemed very sure that she would.

There had been a row, in the restaurant, and Emily had walked out. She had thought that was the end of it. The chance meetings stopped and the circle she and Geoffrey belonged to did not include unsuccessful journalists.

Then she saw him again. She had been in the bar of the golf club, waiting for Geoffrey, and David had come in. He was moving unnaturally, swaying on his feet, and when he came to sit beside her, she saw that he was drunk. She would have left, but it became apparent that she couldn't do so without provoking a scene. For a while he didn't speak to her and then he started to talk in a savage undertone. He said that she was a high and mighty little bitch and did she really think that she was too good for him? There was a lot more and she tried not to listen, watching the door for Geoffrey. He lurched against her, imprisoning her arms by her sides and began to kiss her.

Geoffrey came in with his golfing partner and pulled David away and knocked him down. David had fallen badly, and when he got up from the floor the blood was running from his mouth. He neither moved nor spoke; he stood like a statue and stared at Geoffrey. She had been frightened by the look on his face. But David did nothing. He took out a handkerchief and wiped the blood from his mouth. And then he left the bar.

She said uneasily: "I know to some people it would be an unimportant incident that had been humiliating and silly. But David wouldn't think like that, would he?"

It sounded very slender. I said: "And one way to get his own back on Geoffrey is to run to him with tittle-tattle about his wife? It doesn't sound very effective, does it? David doesn't usually go in for ineffectual gestures of that kind. He's too careful and too proud. It sounds more as if it were you he hated, my sweet. Or me."

She said: "I suppose so." Her eyes avoided mine and she bit at her lip in an embarrassed, unhappy way.

I said: "Why didn't you tell me this before?"

She looked confused. "I suppose I thought it would upset you."

"Did you think I would believe you had been to bed with him?"

"You wouldn't have believed it when I told you it wasn't true. But afterwards, when I wasn't there, you'd have worried about it."

Her voice was cool, matter-of-fact, but her eyes were hurt. I remembered my frequent, small jealousies and was suddenly ashamed, forgetting how well founded they had always seemed to be.

I said: "Darling, I'm sorry. It's only because I have no right to mind."

She smiled: "Tom, have lunch with me?"

I said: "I wish I could. But I told Nora I'd be back."

She didn't smile in the way she usually smiled when this sort of thing happened. Instead she looked weary and the air of health and well-being left her face. I was conscious of the tired, blue shadows under her eyes. At last she did smile, though not convincingly, and said:

"I'm sorry, Tom. But perhaps it would have been a silly thing to do anyway."

I said helplessly: "I love you." And then, as she stood up: "I'll ring you."

It sounded inadequate and foolish: I watched her walk away from me across the bar and out through the swing doors. She moved well with a straight back and long steps. She looked tall and very beautiful.

When I left the hotel I wondered whether to go back to college and fetch my bicycle or whether to catch a bus back to the house. It suddenly seemed to be of immense importance that I should make up my mind correctly. It was ten minutes' walk back to the college; on the other hand, although the buses stopped at the end of my road they moved very slowly through the heavy traffic in the centre of the town and were always crowded at lunchtime. I stood, immobilised with indecision, outside the swing doors and blinked at the sun which was bright after the dark bar and hurt my eyes.

When I saw David he was parting from his group of undergraduates and, left alone on the pavement, was looking at me uncertainly. It struck me, then, that I was not in the least angry with David, nor had been at any point since the telephone call. The absurdity of this amused me and I grinned at him widely, and said:

"Hallo, David."

He looked surprised and faintly relieved. He yawned in an exaggerated manner and rubbed his eyelids squeakily over his eyeballs. He was unshaven and the skin of his forehead was scaly.

I asked him if he had recovered from the party and he muttered something about a thick head. I said that I wasn't surprised and he bared his long teeth and said that he hadn't expected to see me looking so fit.

These civilities accomplished, we stood for a moment or two, drugged by the unexpectedly warm sun. I waited for him to say something about Emily because he must have seen that we were together, but instead he dived into a long, involved and obscene story about one of the town's leading councillors. It wasn't at all funny, and I don't think he expected it to be because he tailed off just before he reached what might have been the point and left the councillor in midair, so to speak, on the road to Brighton with his wife's Swiss maid.

We started to walk together up the street towards the bus stop. We were both silent and David kept his eyes on the pavement so that all I could see of him was his long black hair and broad, hunched shoulders.

At last he said: "Tom, old boy, can you let me have a fiver?"

He had asked me for money before, but never so baldly. There had always been some long-winded explanation of why he needed it and over-loud assurances about paying it back. He had usually done so promptly; he wasn't dishonest about money.

This time it was different. There were no explanations, no promises. The request was made casually, with an air almost of authority. He was watching me with brown, bright eyes and a small, triumphant grin. For a moment or two I didn't understand what was happening and when I did I felt no anger, only astonishment.

I said, without thinking: "David, are you blackmailing me?"

He flushed darkly and screwed up his eyes at the sun. He said: "Come, come, Tom. What a way to treat your brother-in-law." He didn't sound very sure of himself. He began to assume anger. "Is it so unreasonable a thing to ask? You don't have to lend me money, but you've done it before without insulting me. As it happens I'm in a bit of a spot at the moment, but I wouldn't have asked you if I'd thought you'd take advantage of it. I didn't think you'd object."

"Especially after last night?" I wasn't in the mood for evasion or politeness.

He stopped blustering and shrugged his big shoulders in mock acceptance.

"All right. But blackmail's a nasty word, Tom, isn't it? What could I do? Tell Nora about the nice piece you've found yourself? That would put the cat among the pigeons beautifully, but, believe me, old boy, I wouldn't do it. I just appreciate your taste."

He smiled with sly pleasure. "But they're a bad pair to get mixed up with, Tom. Tarred with the same brush. Not the right sort of people for the grammar schoolboy who wants to make good. They can do you a lot of harm."

The slyness had gone from his voice; he sounded friendly and anxious, and almost as though he minded about me. I asked him what he meant.

He said evasively: "Just knowledge of human nature, Tom. Expensively acquired."

Then he grinned in his normal, malicious fashion and said: "Anyhow, I can appreciate your feelings. Don't be deceived by them, that's all. She's a honey, she's lovely, she has magnificent legs. She's an excellent upper-class tart."

His voice was suddenly venomous and his eyes were blank and angry. If I had not been sure, at that moment, that Emily loved me and if she had not told me about David in the bar of the Woolpack, I would have knocked his crooked teeth down his throat. As it was the anger was softened by a kind of pity for him.

I said: "Must you behave like a bastard? It must have given you quite enough vicarious pleasure to tell Geoffrey about Emily and me. A kind of adultery by proxy."

His face was a dark and sallow red. I had never seen David so completely off his guard.

He said: "I didn't tell Hunter anything of the sort. For God's sake, man, what do you take me for?"

He sounded quite bewildered and entirely genuine.

I said: "You were too drunk to remember."

He shook his head. "Not that drunk." He shook his head clumsily as if he were feeling muzzy. The flush grew deeper. "I swear I didn't say anything of the sort, Tom. Why the hell should I? Why should I want to do you that kind of harm?"

"Not me, perhaps. But Emily. You did see him, didn't you, last night? You had a row with him?"

"Oh, we had a row all right. But not about that."

"Did you say anything about Emily?"

He looked confused but only momentarily. Then he said, in his usual defensively cocky manner: "We may have done. I think; it is quite likely that we did."

He looked like a schoolboy with a secret and as if he were enjoying himself.

We had reached the bus stop and I joined the queue.

I said: "I shouldn't try too hard to get your own back on Geoffrey. You might bruise your knuckles."

He chuckled suddenly. "Don't bother about me, Tom," he said. "David's safe on Tom Tiddler's ground."

The bus came and I fought my way on to the upper deck with the school children and the shopping housewives. I found a window-seat and looked out at David. He was standing where I had left him, his legs splayed out and his stomach and bulky chest thrust forward so that he looked truculent and top-heavy. A young man in a college blazer came up and spoke to him; he was a nice-looking boy with flaxen hair and a long-boned, untidy body. David smiled at him and from his eager gestures and moving mouth was clearly trying to impress. He looked short beside the boy, fat and rather old, and suddenly his anxiety to please seemed pathetically childish and a little sad. I remember that I craned my neck forward as the traffic jam eased and the bus moved jerkily away and for some absurd and inexplicable reason tried to keep him in sight for as long as I could.

As I got off the bus the big grey car came out of the turning and swung into the traffic on the main street. It was a shabby pre-war Bentley with a drop head, a nice car, the kind of car I would have liked to own if it had been possible for me to buy a car at all.

Then I remembered that the Hunters had a 1936 Bentley, and I stood at the corner and tried to make out the number-plate but the bus moved off too quickly and the car was gone.

By the time I reached the gate of the house I had forgotten about the Bentley. I was tired and hungry, and I hoped that lunch was ready. It was natural and normal to be coming home and at that moment, as happened frequently, everything that there was between myself and Emily seemed as small and far away as an image seen through the wrong end of the telescope. The little, ugly house looked amicable and pleasant in the sunlight, the dahlias splashed their bright colour in the narrow garden and I had a sudden, happy feeling of security. I was glad to be home.

I suppose I should have known that something was wrong as soon as I went into the kitchen, by the way in which they turned towards me, by the look on their silent, waiting faces. But I was still warmed by contentment; I said, with what must have seemed to them, appalling incongruity:

"Isn't it a lovely day?"

Neither of them answered me and then I saw Nora's face. She was standing by the glass door that led from the kitchen into the garden. She was very white, but as she looked at me she flushed painfully and hotly and put her hand to her mouth.

She said: "Oh, Tom," and her voice was uncertain, almost frightened.

Mrs. Parry was sitting at the table, knitting. The needles clicked monotonously together as if they had a separate and malevolent life of their own. Her grey hair was cut in the clinging bob of the 1920's which made her heavy face look wide and flat.

She spoke with an ominous air of pleased satisfaction.

She said: "We've had a visitor."

Nora caught her breath and began to cry gently, her eyes fixed on my face. I put out a band towards her and she turned away, rejecting me, and leaned her forehead against the glass of the door.

Mrs. Parry said: "Crying's not going to do you any good, my girl." She sounded contemptuous. She looked at me and her eyes were opaque, like brown stones.

"You thought you'd keep it dark, didn't you, Mr. Clever? Carrying on behind our backs, deceiving your wife and having your fun? You never thought you'd be caught out, did you? Oh, no, you were too clever for us. But you weren't quite clever enough!"

My limbs were icy cold and trembly. I said: "Who was your visitor?"

She had a small, shiny mouth with tight-drawn lips. She said: "Mr. Hunter came to see us. He's a very nice gentleman. You could see he didn't like what he was doing, but he felt it was his duty to tell us. He was ever so upset, but he said it was better that we should know about it so that we could put a stop to it. He's too good for that woman he's married to—that sticks out a mile. He tried to stick up for you. More fool he! He tried to make out that it was nothing very much and that it wasn't your fault that it had gone as far as this. We know different, of course, and I told him so."

She snapped her mouth shut and began to cast off the stitches on her needle.

I had a cramp in my stomach. The room seemed very quiet and still. I went over to Nora and touched her arm gently. She jerked away from my hand and looked at me. Her eyes were wet and swollen and her whole face was dirty with tears.

She said, in bewilderment: "Tom, I can't believe it. I can't believe it."

Her face puckered and she began to cry again in a noisy, overwrought fashion. I stood helplessly beside her, wanting to take her in my arms and not daring to do so.

Mrs. Parry put down her knitting and stood up. She was a big, short woman with the same build as her son, stumpy legs and a heavily square body.

She said: "Of course it's true. Just look at him. It's written all over his face. He doesn't like being caught out, does he? Oh, he's a fine one. It's all right for him—he's got you to work and slave for him, keeping his house nice, and he's got that woman too. She's got plenty of clothes, she can afford to go and have her hair done nicely, she can buy his drinks for him—oh, he's sitting pretty. She doesn't have to worry where her next penny's coming from. That's fine for her, and for Mr. Clever Harrington. You picked yourself a fine one, my girl. I told you you should have found yourself a decent working man instead of getting too big for your boots and wanting someone educated.'"

Her voice was false with hideous mimicry. She came up to us, where we stood by the door, and faced Nora with her hands on her hips and a look of ugly, bitter anger.

"It's all my own fault," she said. "I shouldn't have listened to your fine ideas about going to a university. Oh, yes, it sounded all right at the time. You were going to get educated, weren't you, and get yourself a good teaching job with a pension at the end of it? It was going to be well worth not earning for a few years so that you could get better pay when you came out of college? You could have got a decent, honest job like all the other girls, but you were too high and mighty for that. Too good for your own brother, weren't you? Your own brother who had to go out to work at fourteen just so you could stay at school like a little lady—and then you were ashamed of him because he didn't talk the way you thought he ought to and you didn't want him to meet all your la-di-da friends from college. Everyone had to give way to you—I had to work and slave when other mothers took their daughter's earnings and had it a bit easy. Not that I complained about it—I didn't. Then nothing came of the grand job, did it? You got married instead, didn't you? Thought you were doing well for yourself. 'My husband works at the university,' and no one else was good enough to lick your boots. I hope you're pleased now. It's done you a lot of good, hasn't it?"

There was a small trickle of spit running from the corner of her mouth. She struck Nora hard across the face with her open palm.

She wasn't really striking at Nora. She was striking at herself, at her own life, at the empty, mocking years and it was painful to look at her. Her thin mouth was quivering horribly and her eyes were vicious. She stared at Nora and then she turned and lumbered blindly out of the room. Her footsteps went heavily up the shoddy stairs and a door slammed on the landing.

Nora's face was full of astonishment and shame. She was very pale except for the wide, scarlet mark across her cheek and mouth.

She said: "Oh, God," and hid her face on my shoulder. I held her tightly and stroked her hair and let her cry. I felt very tender towards her and infinitely sorry.

When, finally, she was able to talk, it was worse than I had expected it would be. I had expected anger and hysterical reproaches and been prepared for them. But they didn't come. Instead, she said that it was all her own fault, that she'd been a bad wife, that she hadn't been able to help me in my work and that she was desperately sorry. I told myself that the anger and hysteria would come later, but it didn't help. I felt a swine.

She sat on the edge of the kitchen table, her legs dangling, and wiped her eyes with my handkerchief. She said:

"Tom, do you really love her?"

I nodded. "I think so."

Her hair was soft and untidy, her face was pitiful. "Tom, you won't leave me, will you?" she said. "I don't care if you love her. Only please never leave me."

She sounded like a child afraid of the dark.

I said: "Dear Nora, of course I'll never leave you. Why the hell did Hunter have to come?"

She said: "Tom, don't be cross with him, please. He meant to be kind—he was very sweet and gentle—and it was only right, wasn't it? I mean, it was only fair that I should know. It would have been so *dishonest* for him not to tell me."

"Dishonest" was one of her words; now, in this context, it sounded pathetic and adolescent.

I hoped that the anger didn't show in my face. I didn't want to hurt her any more.

I said: "It doesn't matter now. Only it seemed cruel."

She said gently: "But it was true, Tom. Won't you tell me about Emily? I'd rather know."

I tried to explain. It came out haltingly and it sounded petty and shameful. There is nothing that sounds so faked as a remembered emotion. She did her best to be understanding and kind, and I despised myself.

In the end, because it was getting late, we made lunch together. We were clumsy; we burned the sausages and forgot to cook the potatoes so that the meal became a joke, and we laughed at ourselves excitedly as if it were an unexpected picnic. We talked nervously and wildly as if we were both afraid that a silence would mean that words best left unsaid would be spoken. The whole thing became oddly unreal like a bad play in which the scenes are not working out to a conventional pattern and the plot is not convincing enough to make them seem real.

I had forgotten that Sandy would come home for lunch, and I think that Nora had forgotten too, so that his appearance in the doorway shocked us into silence. His fair hair was endearingly long and hung in his eyes, his blazer was torn and his shoelaces untied. He stared at us both through his fringe of hair and flung his satchel untidily on to the table. He frowned at the blackened sausages on his plate and ate them rapidly, with an air of insult. Nora and I avoided each other's eyes; we talked separately to the child in a bright, consciously interested manner that made him look from one to the other with puzzled eyes. He swallowed his stewed apple, and said:

"Stewart's got a bike for his birthday. He's seven. I'll be seven, too. Can I have one?"

I said: "Perhaps. We'll see."

He said: "I'd like a bike. Stewart's Mummy lets him ride in the road. Can I get down now?"

He got down from his chair, hitching his grey trousers round his small hips, and buckled on his cowboy holster. Nora began a protest, doomed from the beginning, about his taking a gun to school to which he listened with silent scorn.

"It's all right," he said. "I'll put it in my desk. No one will see."

He picked up his satchel, Nora combed his hair away from his forehead and scrubbed at the dirty mark round his mouth. He shifted restlessly under her hands, and said:

"That's *enough*, Mummy. I'll be late." And he left the house chanting loudly.

When he had gone we cleared the table and began to wash up in silence. We did not look at each other.

In the end I cleared my throat with a noisy effort, and said: "Nora, dear, I'm not busy this afternoon. Would you like to come for a walk?"

It sounded like a bit of bad dialogue written by an amateur.

She looked at me suspiciously. Then she said: "If you like." Her voice was reluctant.

She went upstairs and I finished the wash-up and put the plates away. When she came back she was wearing the green suit that she had bought in the spring and kept for special occasions. She stood in the doorway looking shy. I told her that she looked very pretty and she blushed self-consciously.

The afternoon was still warmly sunny. By the river the trees were changing colour and the early fallen leaves floated on the stippled surface of the water. We walked a yard apart and talked in short artificial sentences.

Nora was in one of her rare moments of beauty; her features were small and pointed and too pale so that she seldom appeared more than pleasantly pretty and when she looked lovely, as she did now, it was a surprise and a delight. Her skin was soft and clear and flushed and her eyes were bright. I remember that I looked at her with a kind of distant pleasure as I would have looked at any pretty woman, and I felt no more than that. It seemed, then, monstrous that this should be so. From some obscure motive of self-torture or perhaps to startle myself into emotion, I began consciously to evoke a series of sentimental pictures from the early days of our life together. It was entirely an academic exercise, and worthless. It seemed, suddenly, that I did not know her at all, that she was not even a familiar reflection in the mirror of habit, but a total stranger to me.

She said: "Tom, you won't see Emily again? Will you promise me that?"

The face she turned towards me was shut and unsmiling and waiting for an answer. I felt very tired.

She said: "It can't go on, can it?"

I said: "Nora, I can't make that kind of promise. Not now, not this minute. How can I? I shall have to see her again. I owe her something. You can't cut off this sort of thing as if you were amputating a limb."

It was a defence and a kind of appeal. It arose, and this shamed me inwardly, less from my love for Emily than from a sharp fear of making any irrevocable decision. It was not the situation that provoked the fear, it was a long habit and a half-admitted weakness.

She looked at me with a cold, remote bitterness. She said with contempt: "You were never much good at making up your mind, were you? Do you think you can get away with it?"

For a moment she stared at me with a white, controlled anger. Then the lines of her face shattered into misery and she began to cry.

She said: "Tom, how could you do this to me when I loved you so? How could you do it?"

She said it over and over again like an anguished child. And then she said all the things I had expected her to say in the beginning, in a spate of pitiful, stereotyped phrases. She said that I had ruined her life, that I had destroyed her trust in me. That she loved me desperately and that she never wanted to see me again. That she wanted a divorce and then that all she wanted was for us to stay together. It all came out between bursts of weeping; she was walking fast along the river, on the soft, green grass, her shoes dusty among the leaves. Then she stopped and faced me.

She said: "Tom, how can you be so stupid? She isn't worth it. Don't you know that? Don't you know that she's a bitch, that she's done this sort of thing hundreds of times before?" Then the despair went from her face; she looked old and curiously evil. She produced a stream of filthy epithets that I should not have thought she knew.

In the end she said: "It isn't only Geoffrey who knows all about her. Everyone does. You ask David. He knows what she is."

She caught her breath and began to cry again, turning her sad, blotched face away from me. I tried to put my arms around her but she wrenched herself away and ran, stumbling among the fallen leaves. I let her go because there was nothing else I could do.

I watched her, and as I stood there, a memory came unbidden from a forgotten occasion of Nora running through the rain to meet me, her wet hair blowing and her face full of love. I felt nothing, only numbness and cold and an aching kind of regret.

Chapter Four

I went back to college and sat at my desk by the window pretending to work on my lecture notes, watching the sky above the quadrangle darken abruptly and fill with sudden rain. I felt immensely tired; my bones were stiff and wearily aching as though I had just climbed a mountain. I gave up the pretence of working quite early; by the time my scout brought me my tea and switched on the lights, it had been, for almost an hour, too dark to see.

He drew the heavy curtains and said it looked as if it were blowing up for a nasty night, and that you never knew what the weather was going to do at this time of the year. He was a little, chatty man with a face like a friendly weasel and a perpetual, wrinkled smile. He seemed to stay interminably, laying out the tea and putting on the fire, talking all the time with sparrow brightness until my nerves were stretched to breaking point. When he had gone I left the desk and crouched in front of the angry bars of the electric fire, smoking one cigarette after another.

Then I remembered that I was expected at the Fosters' at six-thirty; teaching their crippled child was an act of charity that I suspected in myself and for this reason I never missed his weekly lesson. The boy was the younger brother of one of my bright, working-class pupils; I had taken on the voluntary task with a kind of dedicated enthusiasm, seeing it as a magnanimous act of rescue, half-believing that I should find a quick intelligence that could be sharpened into brilliance. By the time I had realised that the gesture was worthless, that the boy's brain was as handicapped as his body, I had grown so ashamed of my own motives in starting the lessons, of my own deluded picture of myself as a knight in shabby armour, that it was impossible to put an end to them.

I got up reluctantly and went to the sheds for my bicycle. It was raining now, in small cold flurries that stung my face and froze my hands. The roads were slippery and there was no moon. The late, surprising sun of the afternoon had been the last of the summer.

The Fosters lived in a new council cottage near the river. The estate was not yet finished; the roads round the houses were unmade and muddy, and the spoiled fields were littered with lengths of pipe and concrete mixers. The defaced country was hidden by the wet, dark evening and as I turned off the lane on to the new road that led to the houses, their welcoming windows glowed with warmth like oranges on a Christmas tree.

Steven was waiting for me in the front room of the house, his wheel chair drawn up to the table, his hands lying loose on the rug that covered his useless legs. He was a nice child, he had a slow smile of astonishing sweetness and he watched my mouth all the time I was talking to him with a rapt concentration that had at first encouraged me to think that he understood what I was saying. Now I knew that it was an illusion; that he had been told so often that he was a lucky boy because I had offered to come and teach him that he was terrified of offending me by saying that he didn't understand. I had tried, since I had realised his limitations, to force him to tell me when the lesson was too difficult for him. Sometimes I would succeed and he would ask me a question but always, by the next week, he had returned with careful obstinacy to his first habit of sitting in silent, awed stupidity. He was fifteen and he had the mental capacity of a child of ten. I was not equipped to teach him or to help him; the hour that I spent, every week, in the polished parlour was a penance for me and, I suspected, a misery for him. This week I had brought my stamp album with me in the hope that it would help him to learn geography. He turned the pages with cries of pleasure because the stamps were pretty; he listened dutifully to my short monologues and when, at the end of the hour, I said that he might keep the book, his peaky face softened and glowed with such rapture that I felt ashamed. I swung his chair round and he propelled it to the door, opening it with his stick and wheeling himself into the kitchen beyond.

"Look, Mum," he said. "Look what Mr. Harrington's given me."

She put a hand on the boy's shoulder and smiled gratefully at me. She was a big slatternly woman with a kind, worn face.

She said: "It's ever so kind of you, Mr. Harrington. Stevie, did you say thank you nicely?"

He looked at me and hung his head in a confused way.

I said quickly: "Of course he did, Mrs. Foster."

She said effusively: "You're too good, Mr. Harrington. There's not many who'd come and teach Stevie. I'm sure we can never be too grateful, can we?" She smiled gently at the boy and offered me a cup of tea.

I told her that I had to get back and felt my face colour at the lie. It would have been pleasant to sit in the warm kitchen after the cramping cold of the unused parlour, but to-night I felt rather more of a fraud than usual. To sit and listen to her gratitude would have been ari unbearable reproach. She said that of course she understood, that it was too good of me to have given up so much of my time already and that she had no right to keep me any longer. She was regretful about it, and I felt that I had denied her a pleasure.

Outside the wind was stronger than it had been when I came, blowing in chilling gusts of fine rain. I free-wheeled down the rutted road and out into the lane.

I tried to brake as soon as I saw the headlamps of the car sweep the high, grass bank, but the tyres of my bicycle were slimy with mud and would not hold on the tarmac. The big car slewed round the bend in the lane, rocked a little and caught my front wheel with its offside wing. The bicycle frame buckled beneath me and I fell miraculously clear, landing in the narrow ditch with a sharp pain in my groin. The car went by with a rush of wet air; it was a grey drop-head Bentley, and when I saw the letters on the number plates I knew who was at the wheel.

The car was being driven badly; I had heard the brakes whine on the road and she had taken a difficult corner at a speed that was dangerous in the wet and the dark. Geoffrey was by instinct and training a cautious driver; he handled a car in the way that he would have ridden a horse, with solicitous care. I picked myself out of the ditch, angry and scared and sore, and wondered why Emily should be driving down to the river. The lane came to a dead end at the tow path.

Then I knew where she must be going and the knowledge was physically painful, like an unexpected blow. The doubts and the perennial jealousy came back in a flood of sick anger. I picked my shattered bicycle off the road and flung it into the ditch. I began to walk along the lane towards the river. My hands were throbbing with nettle stings. I had pulled a muscle in the upper part of my thigh and limped with the pain.

It was about half a mile to the river. By the time I got there the rain had soaked through my raincoat and dripped off my hair and was running in small streams under my collar and down my cold back. My right trouser leg was torn and flapped damply against my knee. I had forgotten about Nora. I had forgotten about Geoffrey. Nothing and nobody was real or important except Emily and my love for her. And my own bitter, jealous anger.

The Bentley was parked at the end of the lane, one front wheel in the ditch. On the tow path, out of the shelter of the hawthorn hedges, the wind was almost a gale and sobbed like a maddened banshee in the branches of the tall poplars that lined the river bank. The river was high, almost up to the level of the fields, and the creaming lips of the waves were luminous in the darkness. The barge was a heavy dark hulk against a dark and moving sky. It rose and fell with the wind and the water and the ropes that moored it to the bank creaked against the iron bollard.

I went up the gangplank, stepping softly as though I was afraid they would hear me coming. It was an absurd piece of melodrama. If anyone had been expecting me they would not have heard me in the noisy night, and there was no one inside the barge to expect me. There was only a pair of guilty lovers. So my anger had made them; there was no reasoning behind my expectation, only an uncontrolled and almost terrifying emotion. I do not know what

I thought I would see when I opened the cabin door. I suppose a conventionally incriminating scene.

Instead they were standing as far apart as the length of the cabin would allow, more enemies than lovers. Emily had her back against the far wall, the flat palms of her hands outstretched against it, her head flung high and defiant in the general attitude of a tragedy heroine facing the villain of the piece. She looked angry and magnificent. Her hair was wet with rain and darkened to a copper colour. She saw me in the doorway and went scarlet.

David turned at the direction of her eyes. He did not look surprised and the smile on his face was as sneering and as confident as I had ever seen it. His eyes were clear and shining so brightly that they might almost have had tears in them. It was hot in the cabin of the boat; he had discarded his jacket and was wearing only a checked woollen shirt that showed his wide chest and his enormous, rippling shoulders. He looked triumphant and nearly handsome.

I closed the door behind me and shut out the frenzied sound of the night. The barge had been built well and when the door was closed it was dead quiet in the cabin. So quiet that I listened to myself breathing, small quick breaths through my nose that sounded like the wind through dry grass.

The barge lurched gently with the movement of the water and a beer bottle toppled gently to its side on the table, rolled in slow motion to the edge and bounced on the floor with a hollow, soggy sound.

The tension broke. Emily moved from her crucified attitude against the wall and David sat down on the bunk, folded his arms and stared at me. His short legs stuck out in front of him, he wore dirty canvas sandals on his feet and his heavy belly rested on his thighs. He didn't look handsome or triumphant any longer. Just sly and confident and middle-aged.

He said: "Well, Tom. It's an odd night for visiting. I'm more popular than I thought."

I looked past him at Emily. I said: "What are you doing here?"

She moved one hand in what seemed to be a gesture of despair.

The tweed suit she had worn at lunchtime was spotted with rain. Her stockings were wet and wrinkled and I saw, with a kind of distant pity, that her light shoes were sodden and smeared with mud. She couldn't have looked more guilty if I had found them in bed together.

She said flatly: "I had to see David. There was something I had to talk to him about."

She sounded as if she didn't expect to be believed. Her eyes had a dark and glassy look as if she were afraid. She didn't look like a bitch. I told myself that the successful ones never did. I hated her. I hated the beauty of her body and the lying honesty of her face.

I said savagely: "I haven't given you enough time to work out a good story, have I? But perhaps you think it isn't necessary. Perhaps you think I'm fool enough to believe whatever you tell me. You should have remembered, when you told me about David in the Woolpack, that I knew him well. Well enough to know that he wouldn't make a pass at someone he wasn't sure about. David's too proud for that, you know."

The skin felt tight round my eyes. I could hear my own voice as if it didn't belong to me, light and cruel and full of hate. She was staring at me in a fixed, fascinated way, the way a rabbit is supposed to look at a snake.

She said, and her lips moved stiffly as if her mouth were hurting her: "Please, Tom. Please. Don't talk like that."

I said: "For Christ's sake don't cringe at me." I was shouting at the top of my voice and there was a hot, twisted pain in my stomach. It was airless in the cabin and there was a thick, steamy smell of wet clothes.

David said, very softly, very gently: "Now, now, Tom. Remember your manners. That's no way to speak to a lady."

I had almost forgotten that he was there. He had unfolded his arms and was leaning forward, his hands on his knees. The sweat glistened on the bone of his high-bridged nose and the mouth beneath it was thin and sour and smiling.

He said: "This isn't an assignation, Tom. But you're a clever boy, aren't you? Clever enough to spot the lie once it is pushed under your nose. You should have believed me, you know, when I told you to keep clear of her. You should never despise other people's experience, especially when it has been as dearly bought as mine."

I said: "What the hell do you mean? Why is she here?"

He grinned like a fox. "You must ask her yourself, Tom. She's not here to go to bed with me. That's all in the past now, over and finished. And, anyway, I wouldn't want anyone else's leavings. She just wants a favour from me, don't you, dear?"

He looked at Emily, still savagely smiling, his long teeth yellow in the light.

She was blazing with anger and her voice shook.

She said: "Don't listen to him, Tom. He's evil. A nasty little man. Will you please take me home?"

David got to his feet and stood between us. He stared at Emily, the hot blood bright in his face. He was swaying a little with the motion of the boat, his powerful shoulders and thick, lowered neck making him look suddenly menacing, like an angry bull.

His voice was suave and controlled, but with an edge to it like sharpened steel.

He said: "That's what I am, is it? A nasty little man. A nasty, common little man. Not fit to lick your pretty, wellborn feet. You didn't think me so despicable a few minutes ago, did you? It was 'dear David,' then, and how fond you'd always been of me and would I do something for you for an old friendship's sake? Now I'm a nasty little man and you despise me. I don't do what you want, so you don't have to be polite any more. You can say what you think of me because there's nothing to be gained by hiding it. You think you can get rid of me as you got rid of me before. You and your charming Geoffrey. But it isn't so easy this time. I know too much about you. And not only the things you don't want Tom to know."

The lines of her face had softened. She said: "David, stop it. It doesn't hurt me. Don't you see it doesn't hurt me? You're only damaging yourself."

There were bright tears on the ends of her lashes and she was looking at David as if they were alone together. It was the pity that finished him, that snapped the last, frayed cord of self-respect.

He was breathing quickly and noisily. He said, in a thin whisper of a voice: "You bitch. You filthy bitch." He bent his broad back and picked up the fallen beer, bottle by the neck and cracked the base against the table edge.

I had only seen it done once before, in a drunken fight, and the splintering sound of the glass and the wicked look of the jagged bottle took me back ten years to the dirty Whitechapel pub so that what was happening now had the added terror of a familiar nightmare. I saw David's face briefly, the unmasked hatred and the lips curled back from his teeth. He lunged at Emily's face with the bottle. She threw herself sideways and I heard her high, astonished cry, but only as a background to fear, the anonymous scream in the night. I tackled David from behind, my arms round his shoulders. He was stronger than me, a great deal stronger. He twisted round and hit me in the pit of the stomach so that the sick pain came up into my throat. His breath was sour with garlic and I remember that I wrenched myself away from him as much to get away from the smell as for my own safety.

He came after me, head down, punching wildly, his arms flailing like windmills. I had no chance against him, against his weight and his strength, and his desperate anger.

The knowledge of my own weakness defeated me. I was helpless, like a frightened child being beaten up by the school bully. I remember that I didn't try to hit him. All I wanted was to avoid contact with his sweating, powerful body. He punched me in the diaphragm and I went down in a corner, crouching on my knees, my arms up to protect my head.

But the expected blow did not come. I shook the hair out of my eyes and saw that he was lying by the bunk on the far side of the cabin. He was very still.

Emily said, from a great distance: "I think he slipped on the bottle." And I saw it in front of me, rolling gently backwards and forwards on the cabin floor until there was no more impetus to move it and it was still.

I got to my feet. Everything was out of focus and swimming in mist; nothing was real except the agony of trying to breathe again.

Emily said: "Are you hurt?" She was standing near me, her eyes enormous with terror and compassion. I put my arms round her and felt that she was shaking although her voice was controlled and she did not cry. She smelt of damp tweed and it is a smell that I shall always remember with the panic of the moment and the sweet taste of blood in my mouth. I held her tightly and kissed her face and her hair.

She said, in a high, clear voice: "Tom, look at David."

He was lying with one leg twisted sideways; it looked absurdly short and thin and without bones like the leg of a ventriloquist's doll. His arms were flung wide; the hands defenceless, the fingers uncurled. His face was purpling red, he was breathing with an unpleasant, grunting sound. I lifted, him gently and there was blood on the floor where his head had lain. His hands were limp and cold.

Emily said: "Tom, is he going to die?"

I tried to laugh at her. "Don't be a goose. He's just knocked himself out. He isn't as bad as he looks."

She said slowly: "I pushed him, Tom. And he slipped on the bottle. What are we going to do?"

I took the pillow off the bunk and pushed it under his heavy head. I thought of trying to get him on to the bunk, but my limbs felt as if they were made of rubber, and I didn't want to make a fool of myself or to ask Emily to help me.

I said: "We'd better get a doctor." I went over to the telephone and picked up the receiver.

Emily said: "Don't, Tom. Please." I looked at her and she was as white as paper. "Tom, don't you see? He'll have to tell the police."

I didn't understand. I said: "What does it matter? There isn't anything else to do."

The operator answered and I gave her my doctor's number. The bell rang for a long time and all the time it was ringing Emily was watching me from where she was standing by the bunk with a still, pale face. Her hair was dry now and shone like honey under the bare light.

The doctor's wife answered the telephone. She said no, the doctor wasn't in. Who was it, please? . . . Would I leave a message?

I looked at Emily's face and at the rigid set of her mouth. I said no, it was nothing important. A personal matter. I would ring again.

I put the receiver down and Emily exhaled, a long sighing breath. The lines of her face relaxed and she moved to a chair as if a weary burden had been lifted from her shoulders. She looked at me in a stiff, scared way, and said:

"Tom, what are we going to do?"

It was a cry from the dark. I didn't know, then, why she was so afraid although I was half-aware of the extent of her fear and now I began to feel it too. I had counted on Doctor Rogers. I had known him for years and I knew, suddenly, that I was unwilling to face the questions of a stranger, David was Nora's brother and it was my fault that he was lying there. If he were badly hurt a stranger would be suspicious, unwilling to take responsibility. And he might be badly hurt. He might be going to die.

I went over to David and looked at him. He hadn't moved and it seemed as if he were breathing with more of an effort. I remembered that he ought to be kept warm and I took a blanket from the bunk and wrapped it round him clumsily.

Emily said: "Tom, he'll be all right, won't he? You said he'd just knocked himself out. Didn't you? Perhaps we could give him some brandy and bring him round. He wouldn't want anyone to know, would he?"

She was pleading with me. I thought that I understood why and I felt angry and very weary.

I said: "And suppose he isn't all right? Suppose he does need a doctor? That isn't important, is it? It is only important that there shouldn't be any kind of scandal and that nothing should happen to stop Geoffrey getting his seat. You do care about him, don't you? He's more important to you than anyone or anything else. More important than a man's life."

It was stupidly histrionic but I didn't care. It lessened the responsibility to be able to blame her for my own indecision. Her eyes were hurt and I was glad that I had been able to hurt her.

She said softly: "Tom, don't. Please help me. What can I do?"

I said: "For God's sake, how should I know?"

I was appalled at myself and my own uselessness. She was asking me for help and there was nothing I could do. She got up from her chair and went over to the telephone, looking at me miserably.

She said: "Tom, I'm going to ring Geoffrey."

I suppose I had known all along that she would do that.

It seemed to be part of the inevitable pattern. I said, hitting not at her but at my own powerlessness:

"All right. Ring him up. You want him, don't you? You want him to get you out of a mess. He always has, hadn't he? I'm no good to you. I don't know why you don't say it. Go on, ring him up. Run back to Daddy and ask him to mend it for you."

She was angry. It showed in her eyes and the sudden colour of her cheeks.

She said: "You don't give me much choice, do you, Tom?"

She lifted the receiver and asked for the number of her house. I heard the bell ringing and then a click and a man's voice, small and clear.

She said: "Geoffrey, it's important. There's been an accident."

I couldn't bear to listen to what was, in effect, evidence of my own impotence. I went out of the cabin into the small kitchen in the stern. I filled the kettle and put it on the oil stove. I made as much noise as I could so that I wouldn't be able to hear Emily's voice asking Geoffrey for help.

I smoked two cigarettes while the kettle boiled. I made the tea in a greasy aluminium pot and poured out two cups. I carried them back into the room. Emily was sitting at the table.

She said: "He's coming down. He won't be long. The Ford was at the garage. He'll have to knock them up to get it out. The battery was being charged; that's why I came in the Bentley."

I said: "Just like Berry and Co., isn't it? Is he also bringing a picnic hamper? And the butler?"

I sat on the table, lit another cigarette and drank the tea. It was hot and strong and bitter.

She said: "What else could I do, Tom?"

"How should I know? What do you think the clever Geoffrey is going to do, wave a wand? Does he always dispose of your unwanted lovers so neatly? I'm not much good to you, am I?"

It was the same jealous scene that we had had often enough before. Only it was worse now; there was more of an edge to the anger. And Emily did not defend Geoffrey as she usually did. She was quiet. I had never seen her so quiet.

She said: "Tom, I love you. I wanted you to take me away, don't you remember?"

"I let you down, didn't I? You knew that I would; you only asked me because you knew that you were safe. You knew that I couldn't leave Nora and that you would be able to stay with Geoffrey. So that it was easy enough to make your grand gesture. . . ."

Even then I was astonished that love could become so twisted.

She shook her head. "It isn't like that at all. Don't you know that it isn't?" She sounded lost and unhappy. She went on, fumbling for words in a tentative way that was unlike her. "I was stupid, but it wasn't just a gesture. I wanted to come away with you, Tom."

I said: "It doesn't sound as if you made a habit of leaving Geoffrey for your lovers."

"No," she said, "I don't make a habit of it."

She was smiling in a drained, unhappy way and I felt a fool. I said that I was sorry and we sat in silence and waited for Geoffrey. The cabin was quiet except for the noise of David's breathing. It was a noise midway between a snore and a gasp and more regular now. I went to look at him and thought he looked a better colour although his skin was glistening and damp, and he moved his head fretfully on the pillow. I picked up the bottle and the pieces of broken glass and put them into the bin in the kitchen. I washed up the teacups and hung them back on their hook above the stove. Then I went back to Emily and we went on waiting.

He came after an unending stretch of empty time. He stood in the doorway and the wind swept in with a cold rush. Outside, the wind screamed in the poplars. It wasn't a pleasant sound.

He looked tidy and sure of himself. His face was grave, fitting the occasion, and ruddy with cold air.

He shut the door, and said: "Well, you had better tell me about it."

His voice was firm. I felt, both relief that he was there to take the decision, and resentful anger because he was so much more able to do so than I.

Emily said: "After I'd been here for a little while Tom came, and there was a fight. And David fell."

She spoke in a frightened monotone, her eyes fixed on Geoffrey's face. He nodded slowly, not looking at her. I wondered what she had said to him on the telephone, and how she had explained her own presence here.

He said to me: "Why did you come to the barge?"

I said: "I saw the car. It passed me in the lane. I knew it was Emily because she nearly killed me."

His mouth twitched. "I see," he said. "It's good of you to take so keen an interest in my wife's virtue. I suppose I should thank you."

He crossed the cabin and knelt down by David. His back was towards me and I couldn't see what he was doing. When he stood up, there was no expression in his face at all.

Then Emily began to cry. Softly and slowly with her face hidden in her hands. Geoffrey went over to her and stroked her hair, and she leant wearily against him as if she were glad he was there. I was suddenly aware of the extent to which I had failed her.

Geoffrey said: "It's all right, dear. It's all right."

I couldn't bear to watch them together. I said: "Do you want me?"

Geoffrey looked up with cold, surprised eyes. "Oh," he said. "Do you want to go?" He paused inquiringly. "In that case, perhaps you would take Emily home? I'll do what I can for Parry."

Of course he could manage alone. He'd get him into a hospital, if it should be necessary, without any scandal. He was competent and clever, and always successful.

I said: "Of course I'll take her home. I'll wait in the car."

And I slammed boorishly out of the cabin and ran down the gangplank, stumbling in the mud at the river's edge. It was very dark, and I fell against the bonnet of the car before I realised that I had reached it.

At first the car was a haven of stillness and warmth, although, drenched as I was, it was a negative kind of relief. After the first moment or so I was too conscious of my soaked shoes and wet clothes to be grateful for shelter; I huddled my raincoat about me and shivered, nursing the familiar and almost cherished hatred of Geoffrey to me like a child its favourite toy. Present humiliation was an effective spur; I luxuriated with a dry mouth and pounding heart in remote dreams of vengeance.

I don't know how long it was before Emily came. Perhaps ten minutes or a quarter of an hour, although it seemed longer. I know that I had given up consciously waiting for her and wondering what she was doing and why she was taking so long about it.

She opened the door unexpectedly and bundled in, wet with rain and gasping as though she had been blown breathless by the wind. She collapsed into the seat beside me.

She said: "Tom, dear, will you please drive me home?"

Her voice was gentle and tired. Her head was turned towards me; I could see the faint lightness of her hair in the darkness of the car and her shadowed eyes in the pale blur of her face.

I switched on the engine with a sudden excitement that was, incongruously, pure pleasure. I had never driven anything before except a ten-ton army truck, and the controls of the Bentley had a delicate and expensive feel to them. There was a gate into a field on the far side of the lane, and I turned the big car with more success than I had expected. I remember that I was absurdly pleased with myself. I accelerated gently up the lane and on to the main road, changing down with a hideous grating of gears as I slowed at the "Halt" sign. I glanced guiltily at Emily to see if she had noticed my clumsiness, but she was staring straight ahead of her, through the windscreen.

The car was a delight on the main road. It was fast and responsive; the feeling of power relaxed the tension within me. When we were almost back to the town, Emily said in a completely normal voice:

"I could use a drink. How about you?"

I parked the car outside the Goat and Compasses, and we went inside. The saloon bar was empty and warm; we drank whisky and at first we didn't talk to each other. It all seemed surprisingly ordinary as if we had met by chance and were drinking before going home.

Emily was nervously bright. Her eyes were dark and shining and her skin was rosy.

She said: "Tom, what are you going to say to Nora?"

I stared at her like an idiot. I had forgotten about Nora and for a long moment the name meant nothing. Then I was back with a cold splash in the deep end and the water closed over my head.

I said: "Oh, Jesus. What am I going to say?"

She said soothingly: "It's all right, Tom. Say that a lunatic knocked you off your bicycle in the lane and that you had to walk home." She looked at me in a troubled way. "You'd better tell her that you stopped at the Goat and Compasses for a drink. Not with me—or perhaps that's stupid? You'd better say that I was here. That we met by accident and I gave you a lift home. I don't suppose that she'll believe you. But she won't think that it was any more than a guilty assignation."

She grinned at me over her glass with a certain amount of enjoyment. She was riding high on a wave of excitement. I suppose that even then it wasn't too late. The net was not perfect; I could have wriggled out through the hole and swum back to safety.

I said: "And David? He's hardly likely to corroborate this, is he?"

She looked at me. She said: "I don't think he'll want to talk about it."

I said: "You've got it all beautifully pat, haven't you? Did you get your instructions from Geoffrey?"

She didn't answer me, she just went on smiling politely and handed me her empty glass. It didn't occur to me just then that she was only concerned about me, that she was not afraid for herself.

We had another whisky, and then she said: "I'll drive myself home, Tom. I'll drop you at your road."

She was being bright and distant and proud. We went out of the pub and back to the car. She drove to the end of my street and stopped, leaving the engine running. I took the hint and kissed her good night quickly. Her mouth was cold and trembling, and tasted salty.

She said: "Tom, is it going to be all right?" The hard shell had flaked off and she was soft and vulnerable.

I said, because I was still angry: "Don't you know that it will be all right? Geoffrey's in charge, isn't he? Go on, back to your husband with you. He's more use to you than I am."

She didn't speak for a moment. Then she sighed a little, and said: "Good night, Tom. Sleep well. God bless you." And she waited for me to get out of the car.

As soon as the car had gone I was sorry, but there was nothing that I could do about it. I walked home, down Sanctuary Road.

The house was dark and the emptiness hit me as soon as I opened the front door. Nora had left a note. It was scribbled in pencil and heavily underlined. It said that she couldn't bear to be in the house another minute, that they had all gone to stay with her aunt for a day or so. She would write to me. My dinner was in the oven. She was sure I would understand.

Afterwards I was glad they were not there but at that moment I felt, between mounting waves of weariness, only an appalling sense of loneliness and loss.

Chapter Five

I peeled off my wet clothes and had a hot bath. I ate dinner from a tray, smoked a great many cigarettes and wished I had some whisky. I found some brandy that Mrs. Parry kept for medicinal purposes in the bathroom locker; it was surprisingly good and I finished what was left in the bottle.

At about ten-thirty I was drunk enough to ring Emily. She answered the telephone at once; she sounded a little muzzy as if she were already half-asleep.

She said: "Tom? Oh, hallo," in a jerky sort, of way and then there was a pause. I asked about David and she said in a constrained voice that perhaps I had better speak to Geoffrey. There was a mutter off-stage, and then Geoffrey came on the line; I imagined that they were probably in bed together. That was something I usually prevented myself from thinking about; now, having it thrust under my nose, it was a shock to discover how much I minded.

Geoffrey said: "He seemed to be all right when I left him. He came round quite happily and said he didn't want to see a doctor. It seemed to be an ordinary sort of knock-out— nothing much to worry about, anyway. Perhaps you'd go down in the morning and have a look at him." It was an order. His manner was quite kindly but crisp.

I said: "Yes, I can do that."

He said: "That's nice of you. Thanks for ringing." He was distant but quite cheerful as if what had happened on the barge was all in the day's work. Then he said: "I don't think I should tell your wife about it if I were you. It would upset her. And I don't think Parry would like it."

I wondered why he should bother about Nora's feelings.

I said: "I couldn't tell my wife even if I wanted to. She's left me."

He said: "Good God. I'm sorry about that. Let me know if there is anything I can do." He sounded anxious and I had no particular desire to reassure him, so I said good-bye and rang off in a hurry. I hoped the prospect of Nora divorcing me and citing Emily would give him a sleepless night.

My bicycle was where I had left it. There were a couple of small boys playing with it and they scrambled off guiltily when I appeared. I picked it out of the ditch and tried to straighten the frame, succeeding enough to be able to push it. It seemed to be repairable and I propped it carefully against a gate. It was a still, bright morning full of birdsong and the fields and the hedges were clean and washed by the storm.

I met Steven on my way to the river. He was wheeling his chair up the lane and splashing it into the puddles with an air of absorbed interest. He didn't look up until I was level with him.

I said: "Hallo, Steve." He smiled at me shyly and his freckled face went pink with embarrassment.

He said: "Good morning, Mr. Harrington. How are you?"

He was a polite child and might have been a nice-looking one if the skin had been stretched a little less taut over his cheekbones. He usually looked apathetic; this morning he was bright with excitement. I wondered what had happened to him and I talked to him for a moment or two, but he said nothing except in answer to my questions.

In the end he burst out with it, his eyes wide with wonder.

"Mr. Harrington, there's a policeman down by the river. There's someone dead there."

I said: "Have you been to look?" wondering idly how many of the neighbourhood's children were on the tow path watching the police drag a suicide out of the water.

He shook his head and grinned proudly. "No, I haven't just been to look. I took the policeman there. I found him, you see, when I went to fish this morning. I knew he must be dead because he didn't move at all. I came home and Mummy told the policeman on the telephone. And he asked me to take him down and show him."

It was a long speech for Steven. He was breathless and blushing at the end of it.

Mrs. Foster came running down the road that led to the council houses, her long breasts wobbling under her flowered apron, her face distraught.

She said: "Oh, Stevie. Here you are." She looked at me without a smile. "Oh, it's you, Mr. Harrington." And then, to Steven, with the crossness bred from anxiety: "You naughty, naughty boy. I said you were to take the policeman to the river and come straight back. Why couldn't you do what you were told? Driving me out of my mind with worry?"

Steven said: "But, Mum, they didn't mind my being there. The policeman was asking me questions."

She said: "I don't know, I'm sure. You're a bad boy. It isn't a fit place for a child. I don't know what he was thinking about. Go along home with you."

He went reluctantly, manipulating the wheels with his thin, veined hands. She turned to me, her hands at her breast in a wholly unconscious, melodramatic gesture.

"I'm glad they found you, Mr. Harrington," she said. "I told them to fetch you."

I said: "No one fetched me, Mrs. Foster."

"Oh," she said, and her eyes went blank and suddenly shifty. She looked as if she wished she hadn't spoken. She went on hastily: "I'm sorry. I didn't know. I think I'd better get back to Stevie. It's upsetting for him—not being strong, and all that." And she turned and followed Steven in a grotesque, waddling run.

I tried not to hurry down to the river. I felt that somehow it was important not to hurry, to remember that I knew nothing, that I was just a passer by who had been told that there was some excitement on the tow path and that the police were there. It wasn't until afterwards that I realised it would have been more sensible not to have gone at all.

When I came to the end of the lane and the width of grey water, the knot of men round the barge had their backs to me. They stood motionless, looking for a long moment like a still from a film. There were perhaps half a dozen people there, men from the council estate, the policeman and the doctor crouching on his haunches by the gangplank of David's barge.

As I came up to them the men moved aside and I could feel their eyes in the back of my neck and their eager, whispering voices.

David was lying face down, his feet on the boards and his head in the mud at the river's edge. The checked woollen shirt was tawdry bright against the dirty colour of the bank and he had lost one of his plimsolls so that his white, bare foot looked ludicrous and pathetic. One arm was crumpled beneath him; he looked curiously small and somehow empty. I would have known he was dead without the paraphernalia of the police and the gawping crowd.

The things I had meant to say died in my throat. The policeman looked at me inquiringly. I think I said: "He is my brother-in-law."

The policeman said: "I see, sir. I'm sorry. There's been an accident."

He was a big man with curly hair and a shocked, young face. His eyes widened. "Are you Mr. Harrington?" he said. "Mrs. Foster, up at the cottage, told us to get in touch with you. She said you were married to Mr. Parry's sister. Is that right?"

He sounded baffled, a little out of his depth.

I said: "Yes. I seem to have saved you some trouble. As a matter of fact, I came to collect my bicycle. I had a smash last night and left it in the lane. I saw Mrs. Foster and she said there had been an accident by the river."

As soon as I had said it I wondered whether I had explained my presence too eagerly, whether it might not have been better to have said nothing. I remember that I was not at all afraid and that the scene was almost painfully clear and sharply definite so that a long time afterwards I could call it up at will and see the barge and David's dead body and the men standing round it.

The policeman said: "Did Mrs. Foster tell you that it was Mr. Parry who was dead?"

I said: "No, she didn't tell me." I hoped that I sounded like an innocent man.

The doctor got up from his knees. He was elderly, with a narrow, tired face. He said: "He's been dead some time. Can't say anything definite now."

He brushed the mud from his raincoat with nervous fingers. His clothes were fussily neat; he examined his spotted shoes with distaste.

I said: "How did he die?" And he looked at me with weary, distant eyes.

"Really, it's difficult to tell," he said. "You can't give a snap decision in this sort of thing. We shall have to wait for the p.m. before we know the exact cause of death." He sounded a little peevish as if he wasn't used to people who lacked the good manners to die in their beds. He picked up his bag from the bank. "He might have drowned. On the other hand, there's a lesion at the base of the skull. Might be a fracture there. Might be a chronic alcoholic for all I know."

I said: "He wasn't a drunk." And he shrugged his shoulders.

"I wasn't attacking his moral character," he said. "Only answering your question."

It was like scratching a sore spot. I had to go on. I said: "Could a crack on the skull have killed him? I mean, if there is a fracture there?"

He examined me coldly. "It might have done. But damage to the skull is often no indication of the extent of the damage to the brain. Severe brain injuries may exist without any fracture of the bone."

I was in no mood for a medical lecture. I said: "I'm sorry to make a fuss, but the man happens to be a relation of mine."

He looked a little shamefaced. "I quite understand" he said.

Then he took the policeman aside and they stood apart from the group of watchers and talked together. At last the doctor nodded, smiled frostily and went off along the tow path, stepping carefully to the side of the puddles. The policeman came back to me.

He said: "I'm sorry, sir. This must be a shock for you. Finding your brother-in-law like this, I mean. When did you last see him, sir?"

I lied then, more from instinct than from any consciously formulated fear.

I said: "I saw him yesterday. At lunch time. In the Woolpack."

He nodded slowly and scratched his head. "Well, I needn't keep you," he said. He didn't seem very sure what to do next. I had the impression that he would be more at home dealing with a traffic offence.

I said: "What could have happened to him?"

He said helplessly: "*I* don't know, sir. They're usually suicides—in the river. But he doesn't look like a suicide."

After that we hung about silently for a while. There was no point in my staying, but it was difficult to leave. The river was moving gently and the water lapped round David's head with a damp, sucking sound, stirring the wet, dark hair. I wondered how long they would leave him lying there. It seemed somehow blasphemous that he should not be covered with a blanket in the final indignity of death.

I think the sergeant must have felt something of the same emotion; his silence was embarrassed and he moved uneasily from one foot to the other, staring unhappily at the sky.

In the end I said: "I think I'll go along now." It sounded forced and out of place, but there seemed to be nothing else to say.

He looked startled, as if he had forgotten I was there.

He said: "What? Oh, yes, sir. Can I have your address? In case we need to get in touch with you."

He wrote it down in his notebook and thanked me solemnly. I took one last, self-conscious look at what remained of David and walked away. As I turned into the lane a police car swept by me followed by a closed van and the calmness deserted me. I stood still for a moment engulfed in wet, shivering fear and then I forced myself to walk up the lane to where I had left my bicycle. I tried to tell myself that it was important that I should act normally, that I had lied and that I had to stick to the lie. That whatever had happened to David I was morally innocent, that I had not hit him, that I had only acted in self-defence. It didn't help; by the time I had reached my bicycle and began to push it home, I had begun to feel that the net was closing round me.

I stopped at a telephone box on the main road and sent a telegram to Nora. I remember that I was distantly amused at my conventional phrasing. I only said that there had been a serious accident and that David was badly hurt.

There was a long stretch of dreary main road back to the town. I had gone about half a mile when the police car stopped in front of me and the sergeant got out. He was alone in the car except for the driver and he looked very young and anxious.

He said: "Beg your pardon, sir, but you said you had an accident last night."

He looked at my bicycle with a professional air. "That bike's had quite a bashing," he said appreciatively. "How did it happen?"

I said carefully: "I rode into a car." I explained where it had happened and what I had been doing there. He listened politely and said:

"What time would that have been?" I told him and he said: "You know, you should have reported it."

I tried to make a joke of it. "It didn't seem worth it. After all, I wasn't killed."

He was unamused. He said reproachfully: "Didn't you take the number of the car? Can you remember what it looked like?"

I said: "It was very dark and raining. It was difficult to see. I think it was a big car. It might have been a van. Anyway, it was as much my fault as the driver's."

He nodded slowly. "Well, being as you weren't hurt, I suppose it's all right. Only this sort of thing really ought to be reported." He seemed happier now than he had been by the river, as if he was on his own ground.

He said: "Well, I'm sorry you've been troubled, sir."

We smiled at each other and he got back into the car and drove off. I watched him go with a feeling of sweating relief, wondering how soon it would strike him that there were no houses between the council estate and the river, and no habitation that could be reached from that part of the tow path except David's barge. I felt the bicycle was somehow incriminating; I stopped at the nearest shop and left it there, the mechanic shaking his head over the buckled frame saying that it would take at least a week to repair, that it was an out-of-date model so that spare parts were difficult and that it would never be the same again.

I rang the college and told the porter that I would not be in; I gave the impression, I think, that I was unwell although there was no reason why I should not have told the approximate truth. Perhaps, having already lied, it seemed safer to continue to do so.

I caught a slow, jolting bus out to the village. The main street was calm and bright although there was a frosty look to the sun and the conductress said she didn't think that the fine weather was going to last.

I saw Emily before she saw me. She was coming out of the house with a shopping basket on her arm; she hesitated on the pavement, crinkling her eyes at the sky. I liked to watch her when she did not know I was there; there was a kind of excited pleasure in knowing how she looked when she was alone. For a moment I was happy in looking at her and knowing that I loved her; then she turned and saw me and the happiness was gone. Now that we were aware of each other, loving her was no longer a simple and uncomplicated joy. I knew suddenly that I didn't want to have to tell her about David because I loved her and didn't want to frighten her. And this, in a way, meant that I wished I were not with her or that I didn't love her.

She smiled and I said quickly before there would be too much happiness to destroy:

"David's dead."

She looked at me without understanding. Then the lines of her face stiffened, and she said: "Dead? Tom, how do you know?"

I said: "I saw him. There's no mistake. He's dead."

Then, because she continued to stand so still and people passing were beginning to look at us curiously: "For God's sake let's get off the street."

She jerked into movement and began to fumble for the latch key in her handbag. She had some difficulty with the lock as if her fingers were shaking. Finally, she opened it and we went inside.

In the morning-room she turned and faced me with incredulous eyes. She said, her words breathless and unfinished: "How did you find him? Have you told anyone? What did you do?"

I said gently: "There wasn't anything to do. The police were with his body when I went down to the river."

She said, bewildered: "But how did they find him? How did they know he was dead? And why the police?"

I said: "He wasn't in the barge. He was outside, lying on the gangplank. A child found him there."

Her mouth went suddenly shapeless, like an old woman's mouth. She said stupidly: "But I don't understand. How did he die?"

I said: "I don't know. His face was in the water. It looked as if he cracked his skull when he fell last night."

She sat down on the arm of a chair in a boneless way as if her legs would not support her.

"But why should he be there—outside the cabin? Could he have walked there, and fallen?"

I said: "I suppose so. I don't know. There was a doctor there. He said they would find out at the post-mortem how he died."

There was no beauty in her face any more and she might have been any age from thirty to sixty.

She said: "Tom, did we kill him? Oh, my darling."

It was something I had tried not to think about. Now, in the face of her obvious terror, I was not as afraid as I had expected to be.

I said: "I don't know." I fumbled for words of comfort. "Dearest—whatever happened—it was an accident. If he was all right when Geoffrey left him, what else could we have done? If he got sick or dizzy afterwards, when he was alone, and went outside—then we are only distantly to blame."

I didn't believe it and from the way she looked at me she didn't believe it either. For a long, frightening moment we looked at each other almost with enmity and then she got up and came across the room, into my arms. It seemed then that I felt a complete and passionate longing that I had never felt before.

When she drew away and looked at me, her eyes were soft and not frightened any more. Then she said: "Tom, we shall have to tell Geoffrey."

I was grateful for that "we." I said: "It would come better from you. Is he here?"

She said: "In the study, I think. Shall I go and fetch him?"

As soon as she had gone, I felt empty and deprived. I walked about the room, straining to hear Emily's returning footsteps, half-hoping that she would not be able to find Geoffrey and that we could be alone together a little longer. I wondered what Geoffrey would say when she told him and whether he would take control of this situation too.

When they came he looked calm, but his eyes were tired and oddly withdrawn.

He said: "Emily's told me. What did you say to the police?"

It was abrupt, even for him. He took out his pipe and began to fill it, spilling loose tobacco out of his pouch on to the floor with an unusual, nervous clumsiness.

I said: "I didn't tell them I had been to the barge last night."

He said: "Thank God for that, anyway." He went to the drink cupboard in the corner of the room and poured out three glasses of Scotch.

I said: "It's nice to be able to afford to drink yourself out of a gloom."

He grinned a little sourly. "You don't have to join me," he said.

We emptied our glasses in silence and then Geoffrey filled them up again. The whisky tasted sour and I felt that I could drink a bottle without it having any noticeable effect.

Geoffrey said: "I suppose he got out of his bunk and collapsed outside. Didn't the police have any idea what might have happened?"

I said: "No. If the doctor knew, or guessed, he wasn't saying.

72

He was standing very hard on his professional dignity. Was David really all right when you left?"

A little tic had started at the corner of his left eye. He said: "How should I know? He seemed to be well enough. A bit dazed, perhaps, but quite rational. I wanted to fetch a doctor but he insisted that he didn't want to see one. It struck me that he was pretty ashamed of the whole business and only anxious that it should be forgotten as quickly as possible."

Emily sounded puzzled. "But Tom said that he had hurt his head badly." She looked beautiful again and moderately composed.

Geoffrey looked at her. "Head injuries are tricky things. I remember we had a fellow at school who was knocked on the head by a cricket ball. He acted a bit silly for a moment or two and then he went on playing as if nothing had happened. He collapsed and died the next morning during prayers."

I wondered why he was being so affable.

Emily said: "But if it was the bang on the head that killed him, what would happen if the police found out we'd been there?"

Geoffrey leaned back in his chair and examined the whisky in the bottom of his glass. He spoke slowly, in a deliberately judicial voice.

"I would say that it puts Tom in a tight corner. It wouldn't be murder, of course, because from what you've told me it was Parry who started the ball rolling, but I suppose they could get him on a charge of manslaughter."

I knew, then, why he was being so friendly and social. He was enjoying himself. He smiled at me from his unassailable position; the look in his eyes was faintly malicious.

Emily did not move. Her voice was light and strained. "But he fell," she said. "He slipped on the bottle. Tom didn't hit him. Not once. And if he had done, it would have been in self-defence."

Geoffrey stared beyond me, at the wall. "I don't know that it would make all that much difference, dear. Tom would still be held responsible. Oh—I expect he'd get off pretty lightly, but he's already queered his pitch a bit by lying to the policeman. Not that I blame him for that—I'd have done the same thing myself, in similar circumstances. Why put your head in a noose if you don't have to?"

My mouth was dry. "A remarkably unpleasant image, isn't it?"

He smiled. "Sorry, old chap. Clumsy of me." His eyes were wide and blue and shining with surprised amusement.

I said: "Do you propose to tell the police what happened last night? Because if you do I should like to get my story in first."

Emily was on her feet. She was very white. She said: "Of course he isn't going to tell the police. He wouldn't dare. And if what he says is true, then it was me who killed him and not you. I pushed him and he fell."

This sort of stupidity could go on for ever. I said: "David slipped. It was an accident. But he was fighting me, not you. If anyone is to blame, then I am."

Geoffrey tapped out his pipe in the ash-tray. He got up from his chair and stood in front of the fire looking tall and handsome and very much in command. He cleared his throat.

"Look here," he said. "There's no point at all in working out who is to blame. There is no reason why the police should ever know that either of you were there. I don't pretend to know what the legal consequences would be if they found out; that is a risk we must be prepared to take. I think that we should all be concerned to see that they do not find out."

He looked at his shining shoes and then at the ceiling. He might have been on a platform, making a public speech.

"I know that I must sound as if I am evading my duty as a citizen, but this is an exceptional situation. I think, that as long as our consciences are tolerably clear, it would be reasonable to say nothing."

I said: "You like to have things every way, don't you? You don't want your wife mixed up in a manslaughter charge and you manage to make it sound as if it were your moral duty to withhold information from the police."

His eyes creased with laughter and his face broke suddenly into one of his rare, enchanting smiles.

"Come, Tom," he said. "Did I sound so pompous? I'm sorry. But the need for self-justification is a fairly common one, isn't it?"

I felt like a rebuked, small boy. He went on in a light and cheerful voice. "And it is to your advantage, isn't it? A scandal of this kind would affect your career as badly as it would affect mine. We're all in it together; the least we can do is to be civil to each other."

I didn't feel like being civil. "All right," I said, "so we're blood brothers. In that case I would like to know what Emily was doing on the barge."

He looked at Emily with a smile of kind inquiry. Her face was colourless and as blank as an empty page.

He said: "Dear, will you tell Tom why you went to see Parry last night?"

Her voice was brittle. "I would rather not talk about it," she said.

Geoffrey gave me a wry grin. He said: "It's quite simple, Tom. We knew Parry when we were in Belfast during the war. At least, Emily knew him. He was a friend of her brother's. Emily was seeing more of him than I liked and I had to take rather a tough line. A word or two in the right quarter and Parry had to pack his bags and look for work elsewhere. Not the sort of thing I enjoy doing, you understand; but it appeared to be necessary in this case."

He looked rueful as though getting people the sack was the normal, painful duty of a gentleman.

He went on: "Of course it was all tactfully and carefully done. I had no idea that Parry had found out what had happened. It was natural enough for him to feel pretty vindictive towards me when he did. It was unlucky that we found ourselves living in the same town. I think Parry thought he could get his own back in that nasty little column he runs. . ."

Emily said: "Promiscuous wife of prospective Conservative candidate. Is that what you're getting at?"

She sounded extraordinarily bitter.

He said indulgently: "Hardly that. But your little *affaire* with Tom had given him a line, hadn't it?"

I said to Emily: "Was David your lover?"

I didn't mean to be deliberately cruel; the question, at that moment, was prompted more by bewilderment than jealousy.

Geoffrey laughed. "Come, now, Tom. This is hardly the place or the time for that kind of question. Emily thought that there had, at one time, been sufficient friendship between her and Parry for her to persuade him to hold his tongue—or his pen."

It sounded thin and evasive. Emily wouldn't look at me. She sat down and stared into the fire. I wished we were alone together so that I could tell her it was all right and I loved her.

Then I remembered about the bicycle; it was an unlikely thing to cause trouble and, telling them about the sergeant's curiosity, it sounded more of a joke than anything else.

Geoffrey smiled in a pleased sort of way, and said: "There was a nasty scratch on the wing. But the car was due to be resprayed anyway, so I took it along to the garage this morning." He looked at his watch. "I have a lunch appointment. Would you like a lift back into town?"

Emily came to the door and saw us into the car. She smiled good-bye, but her face was tired and withdrawn and it was like parting from a stranger.

We drove most of the way in silence; as we got to the outskirts of the town Geoffrey said: "How has Nora taken this business, Tom?"

I said: "I don't know. I told you last night. She's left me."

He grunted something under his breath and then he said: "She's not thinking of doing anything dramatic, is she? You know—if she were—I can't pretend that it wouldn't be most unfortunate for me."

I said: "I have no idea what she intends to do."

He looked at me side-long. "Look, old boy, if there's anything I can do I'd be pleased to do it. Women will quite often listen to reason from someone else, you know."

I said: "It's kind of you. I'm pleased you should be so concerned with my matrimonial affairs."

He lifted the corners of his mouth in an attempt at a smile but the prominent eyes were cold.

He said: "I seem to be fairly closely concerned in them anyway, don't I? And this morning the bond between us would appear to be even more closely tied. I think we should help each other, Tom."

Of course he had the whip hand. It was useless to pretend anything else.

I said: "All right. If I want your help, I'll ask for it. Will you drop me at my college?"

He stopped the car outside the gate, nodded to me in a friendly fashion and drove away. I stayed in my room until after tea. Then I walked home and found a policeman and a plainclothes man waiting for me there.

Chapter Six

The inspector was a small man in a shabby raincoat. He had a deferential air and a thin face with a delicate, sad mouth. His eyes were bright and the colour of pennies; they slanted upwards when he smiled and gave his brown face a Chinese look.

He was smiling as I turned in at the gate. His voice was flat and harsh and bred in the Midlands.

He said: "Mr. Harrington? We were afraid we had missed you."

I felt as cold as the grey and empty sky. I mumbled something about working in college and he stood politely aside so that I could open the door. I saw the twitch of my neighbour's curtain out of the corner of my eye; ridiculously, I was anxious that we should get inside the house before they arrested me and my fingers were slow and clumsy.

The house smelt fusty and shut up. I took them into the front room, and it seemed very small and cramped with the three of us standing there.

He said: "I'm sorry to trouble you, Mr. Harrington. We wanted to ask you a few questions.

He was casual and bright and friendly; the rosy-skinned sergeant took out his notebook and stood there, waiting like a policeman in a play.

The Inspector said: "We won't keep you long," and smiled again, crinkling his bracken-brown eyes. I knew then that it was all right, that it was only routine and I need not be afraid. And curiously, once the tenseness of fear had left me I did not feel relieved, only soft and spongy, like a marshmallow.

He was un-endowed with the majesty of the Law; he had an air of authority but it was limited, like a bank clerk's. He was entirely unremarkable except for the brightness of his eyes and the exceptional, fine-boned beauty of his hands. They were small for a man, long-fingered and narrow across the knuckles. They were gentle, civilised hands. All the time we were talking they lay still and folded one above the other in his lap.

He said: "Mr. Harrington, I am afraid you must have had a shock this morning. Your brother-in-law . . . Do his family know?"

"I sent a telegram," I said. I felt in my pocket for my cigarette case. It was empty and I took one out of the box on the mantelpiece, lit it and drew in the smoke so deeply that it hurt my lungs.

He nodded. "We shall need to see them," he said. Then: "Did you see him last night?" His voice was patient and inquiring, the question, casual.

I said: "No. I hadn't seen him since lunchtime. I told the sergeant so."

There was a white ridge of skin on his forehead, just below the hair line where his face had been shaded from the sun. He said: "I see. You were at the Fosters' last night, weren't you? What time did you leave?"

I told him and he pursed his mouth gravely. "Where did you go after that?"

I told him about the accident. I said that I had had to walk home. I said that I had dropped into the Goat and Compasses for a drink. He listened.

Then he said: "Can you remember anything about the car that knocked you down? Your bicycle was badly buckled, so the sergeant told me."

I tried to sound rueful. "I wish I did. It'll be an expensive job putting it right again. It was a biggish car—but beyond that I can't help you."

I wasn't sure whether he believed me or not. He asked me a few more questions about David and his family, and then he thanked me and stood up.

"We won't take up any more of your time," he said. His smile was sudden and unexpectedly sweet; it transformed his face. I took him to the door and in the narrow, dark hall he turned and said:

"Was your brother-in-law a quarrelsome man, Mr. Harrington? The sort of man likely to pick a fight?"

I could feel the pulse in my throat. I said, as evenly as I could: "I didn't know him well. We had very little in common."

He looked understanding and said nothing. I said, because I had to know: "I thought it was an accident. Could it have been anything else?"

He said: "What?" as though he had only half-heard me. Then he gave a short, formal laugh. "Oh. Yes. An accident. Didn't it seem like that to you?"

He thanked me again and said good-bye, and walked up the path a little ahead of the policeman. From the back, his thinness gave him an air of pathos; his shoulders looked forlorn and slightly bowed as though he found the world too much for him. When they were outside the gate, he turned and latched it with slow care. It was an ill-fitting gate and he was the first person for a long time who had bothered to close it properly.

When they had gone I lit another cigarette and poured myself a glass of beer. I was sick with relief; I told myself that I had acted like a fool. I should have expected the police. They were only doing their job; David was dead and it was their business to find out how he had died. I wondered if it would have been better or worse if he had died quietly tucked up in his bunk where Geoffrey had left him.

I finished the bottle of beer and picked up the telephone.

Emily was in. It was a bad line and it was difficult to hear everything she said because of the ridiculous gremlin noises. I told her that the police had been, flatly and without preamble. I remember that I waited, almost eagerly, for her reaction. Perhaps subconsciously I was already wary.

She sounded astonished. "Tom, how awful. . . . Will they come here? What shall I say if they do?"

I said: "I shouldn't think they will. After all, I was the obvious person. You and Geoffrey are safe enough."

Her voice was subdued. She said: "I'm sorry, Tom," as though I had deliberately rebuked her. Then, hesitantly: "Tom, I want to see you: May I come over? Geoffrey isn't here. He's gone to London—he had to see a man and he didn't want to put it off."

I said: "Of course. Please come. I'll be waiting."

There was no way to stop her coming, other than telling her the truth. And I didn't want to admit that I minded about the neighbours' gossiping; it would sound shabby and stupid and she would not have understood.

I went upstairs to change my suit and wash. My shirt was soaked with sweat and my hands were clammy. I splashed cold water over my face, looked at my chin and wished I had time to shave. From the bedroom I heard the car drasw up outside the gate and Sandy's voice. I went to the window and saw Mrs. Parry getting out of the taxi. She was looking up at the house; her face was lifted towards me like a pale, malevolent flower.

I wondered if I could get to the telephone before they paid the taxi; I ran downstairs and bolted into the sitting-room. I heard the key turn in the front door before the operator had answered the urgent ringing; I put the receiver down guiltily and went to meet them.

Sandy was grubby from the train journey and his socks sagged round his ankles. His face was alight at being home again.

He said: "Hallo, Daddy. Auntie gave me some lettuce for my garden." He dragged a screwed-up seed packet from his pocket and held it out triumphantly. "I'm going to plant them now," he said, and disappeared through the kitchen to the garden.

Nora didn't smile at me. She was pale and her eyes were pink and narrowed with weeping.

She said: "We came as soon as we got the telegram. I rang you from London, but you were out."

She went into the front room and Mrs. Parry followed her. They looked at me silently, on their faces there was expectancy and a kind of outrage.

I told them about David. There was conventional horror and dismay and a few, undistressing tears. Clearly it seemed, from the arrival of the telegram they had expected to find him dead; now, even the manner of his dying did not appear an additional disaster.

Mrs. Parry said: "He's had it coming to him a long time. Always was quick-tempered, like his father."

Nora said: "What do you mean? Poor Dai . . ." Her voice cracked harshly and the tears flowed again, but more from hysteria than grief. She had never felt, for David, even an apathetic, sisterly affection and I think she must have sounded hypocritical, even to herself, because she wiped her eyes, took out her compact and began to powder her nose.

I said slowly and carefully: "It was nothing to do with quick temper. It was an accident. There was no one else there."

Her voice was contemptuous with disbelief. "And what do you know about it? Do you expect me to believe that he fell and killed himself? My David was as sure on his feet as a cat."

I said: "I only know what the police told me. He might have slipped on something." I remembered the bottle that I had tidied away in the ash bin. I knew suddenly and fearfully that I must be careful not to say something that I should not have known.

She stared at me and I felt myself grow stiff with panic. Then the tension died and she went out of the room without a word, her back set and broad under her black, cloth coat. I went after her wondering if I should say something, but she climbed the stairs slowly and did not look back at me although she must have known that I was there. Her legs were thick and clumsy in elastic stockings and she leaned heavily on the banister rail like a very old woman uncertain of her steadiness and strength. She went into her room and closed the door; for the first time I felt a kind of pity for her and wondered what she felt when she was alone, and how she looked without the familiar mask of bitterness and rancour.

Nora had made up her face untidily; she had put on too much lipstick and it looked absurd and clown-like against the pallor of her skin. She was sitting on a hard chair in front of the window, her hands primly folded in her lap. Her eyes were inimical and defiant.

She said: "I didn't want to come back. If it hadn't been for David, I shouldn't have come back at all."

It wasn't true, of course. She was making a virtue of necessity and at any other time I might have been touched by the bravado and the unhappiness behind it. But now I was listening for Emily with a mixture of fear and excitement; there was nothing I could do to avert calamity and this, in a way, was a kind, of relief.

There was a slender chance. I said: "Nora, dear, I'm sorry but I have to go out. It's important. I'll be back as soon as I can."

She was angrily surprised. "It must be very important for you to leave me now, when my only brother has been killed."

I said patiently, although it was probably stupid to bother: "Dear, he wasn't killed. They're not sure, but it looks as if he fell."

She was barely listening. She said: "It was a terrible way to die. Alone and in the dark. Don't you care at all? Poor Mother. . . ." She was working herself into hysteria; the skin was stretched tight round her mouth and at the corners of her eyes. "Tom, I must talk to you. You can't go out and leave me. Please, Tom . . ."

And then I heard the squeal of the Ford's brakes. They sounded shatteringly loud in the silence although Nora glanced over her shoulder at the window with no more than ordinary, abstracted interest, before she turned back to me.

The whole thing became suddenly a nightmare. I was cold throughout my body with the kind of paralysed fear that comes not with threatened violence but with embarrassment. Embarrassment of that special kind that stems from not knowing how someone whose bed you have shared for eight years is going to behave. I looked at Nora and was afraid both for her and of her. If she had been a stranger it would not have mattered that she was unpredictable. As it was, I found her terrifying.

The gate squeaked open and then the doorbell rang.

Nora sighed and got up crossly from her chair.

I said: "I'll go. Stay here, Nora. Please."

She turned to me an innocent, blank face. She stared for a

moment and then the innocence went and she looked secretive and sly. She said: "Oh, I see. Then you'd better go, hadn't you?"

Her face went slowly scarlet as if with shame. She said, in a mumble: "You won't let her come in, will you?"

"No," I said. "Nora . . ." And I stopped. There was no point in telling her the truth; that I hadn't expected her back. There was no point in saying anything at all.

She ran, pushing past me, into the hall. The tears, genuine and unforced now were running down her cheeks. She went into the kitchen and closed the door behind her. I knew where she would go because it had so often been her refuge at the end of a row—there was a small glass structure leading off the kitchen and it was there she always hid, among the deck-chairs and the paint pots, intentionally forlorn, until she was found and comforted.

I opened the front door and it seemed ridiculously inept that Emily should smile at me with untroubled pleasure. I told her that Nora had come home and the smile went from her face.

She said: "Oh, God. I'll go, then. I'm sorry, Tom."

I said: "It's a bit late to be sorry," suddenly almost viciously angry with her, blaming her unfairly and stupidly, for Nora's hurt, white face.

She said helplessly: "How could I know?" turned sharply and walked back to the car. I ran after her and said that I was sorry, that I hadn't meant it. She smiled at me in a brittle fashion and got into the driving seat. I felt furtive and, I think, that she did too; I remember that we spoke in whispers as if the whole street were listening.

She said, her hand on the parking brake: "Are you coming, Tom?" There was no appeal in her voice, only a flat question. Her lips were still parted in a stiff and stagey smile.

I said: "I can't leave Nora like this. She'll expect me to go and find her."

She said coldly: "Do you always go after her when she runs away?"

I said miserably: "I'm responsible for her."

There was a kind of bleak impatience in her voice. "What else

84

have you to say to her, Tom? You must make it worse for her, just by being there."

I couldn't explain to her that it wasn't as simple as that; she could say that Nora would be better off without me and I could believe her, but it didn't make any difference because Nora, didn't think so too. She wouldn't have understood that Nora would rather have me there as a sounding board for bitterness and anger than not have me there at all.

She started the engine and slammed in the clutch. Sanctuary Road was a dead end; by the time she had turned and come back, I was waiting for her on the other side of the road.

I had thought she was asleep but she turned her head on my crooked arm, and said:

"Tom, did we put the lights on in the car?"

Her voice was sleepy and slurred, the light from the electric fire outlined the curve of cheek and shoulder in pale bronze. She smiled at me peacefully and slowly, and stretched herself like a cat.

She said: "I like to see you looking happy."

I said: "The car lights are on. And I am happy. And I love you."

We whispered, not because anyone could hear us through the thick college walls, but because we were used to whispering.

She said: "What is the time?"

I held out my arm so that I could see my wrist-watch by the fire's light.

"Nearly nine o'clock, perhaps we should go back," I said. There wasn't enough light to see the expression in her eyes; they were too darkly shadowed. But she was staring at me and her voice was suddenly high with fear and wide awake.

She said loudly: "Tom, I don't want to go back. Please don't make me go back." She was stiff and shaking along the whole length of her body and then she began to sob in a hard, dry, childish way so that I found myself soothing her as I would have quietened Sandy if he had woken from a bad dream. She had never behaved like this before, so near hysteria and it alarmed me. It had always seemed that she walked sure-footed through places where I habitually stumbled. I had expected strength from her and support; now, suddenly, the roles were reversed and I was too bewildered to help her. I murmured words of attempted comfort and stroked her hair until she lay still and quiet again.

She said: "I mean it, Tom. I don't want to go back. I'm afraid."

"And I thought you were never frightened."

She whispered: "I don't want to go back."

I said, disbelieving: "You aren't frightened of Geoffrey?"

She said nothing but curled her arms round my neck and hung on to me like a drowning man.

I said inadequately: "What do you want to do? Is there someone you could stay with for a while? A girl-friend—or your aunt in London?"

The grip of her arms relaxed: Her voice had no life in it. "I'm sorry, Tom. It was silly of me. Of course I must go back."

And she pushed me gently away, got up from the couch and began to dress, her face turned away from me.

When I turned on the light she looked pale and almost ill. It was more than ordinary tiredness, her eyes had a dull look to them and her cheeks had lost their roundness so that you could see how she would look when she was middle-aged. Her voice had an edgy brightness.

She said: "Come home with me, Tom, and have a drink. Geoffrey won't be back. You could get a taxi home from the village."

Her assumption that I could afford to take taxis was normally something that annoyed me; now I was too worried by her air of illness to feel even a passing irritation.

We walked in silence to the car; she got into the driver's seat and leaned over and unlocked the passenger's door.

She said: "Tom, how long can you keep it up? This intolerable compromise?"

She spoke with immense and unexpected anger; the car started with a violent jerk that made me bang my head on the windscreen.

I said defensively: "I don't want to keep anything up. But I can't take you away with me. Oh, God, don't you know that I want to?"

She was talking very fast and rather low so that it was an effort to hear her above the noise of the traffic.

"Does it really help Nora to have you there, knowing that you love me and would rather be with me? What do you think it will be like if you stay—in that little house where you can't get away from each other? What are you trying to do, after all? Keep your respectability or your own good opinion of yourself? And for what purpose?"

I said: "There is the child."

Her voice was hard and unnatural. "I know there is the child." She hesitated for a moment and then she went on, talking still rapidly but more clearly now. "I was brought up by parents who didn't want to be together and it is something that no child should have to bear, I was lucky, too. We had a big house with plenty of rooms so that they could spend their days working out ways of living without being in the same room together more than was necessary. When they were together, they quarrelled. I used to lie awake at night, waiting for them to shout at each other. If I could hear them talking I used to pray for them to sound friendly."

She had never talked to me of her childhood before. I can't remember what I said in reply; I suspect it was remarkably inadequate. It was impossible to argue with her without sounding priggish. In the end I said the only thing that seemed to be important then; that I couldn't leave Nora while she still wanted me to stay with her.

She said, quite gently now: "I'm sorry, Tom. I know how you feel. It is just that I suddenly needed you so—will you forgive me?"

I said: "You must forgive me instead." And she took her hand from the wheel and held mine so tightly that it felt as if the bones would crack.

By the time we reached the house the anger had gone, leaving a glow of colour in her face so that she looked beautiful again.

Emily opened the front door with her latch key. We had no warning; when we went into the little morning-room the police inspector was there, waiting with his back to the crackling, bright fire.

His eyes shone like brown water in the light, the skin was stretched tightly across his, narrow face. His raincoat was spotted with mud; he had the air of a bank clerk who had run to seed.

He said, smiling gently: "Good evening, Mrs. Hunter. I am sorry to bother you so late in the evening. We were hoping to find you in at a more convenient hour."

He looked past Emily at me with no sign of recognition on his face at all.

She said sharply: "What do you want?" And her shoulders stiffened as if she were preparing for a blow.

He said: "We are making inquiries about Mr. Parry's death. We were hoping that you might be able to help us."

Her voice was thin and cold. She said: "Of course, if I can help in any way ..."

His eyes wrinkled with his sudden smile. He looked deliberately at me. Emily turned. She said: "Oh ... perhaps you would come into the study? Tom, will you find yourself a drink?"

She went out of the room ahead of the inspector and the policeman; they crossed the hall and the door of the study closed behind them.

Chapter Seven

I had finished my fourth whisky when I heard the front door slam. Emily's footsteps came back across the hall; she opened the door and closed it behind her, leaning against it wearily, as if she had come to the end of her strength. I think she would have fallen if I had not gone to her and put her in a chair.

She looked up at me with a spent, shocked face. I gave her a whisky, and she drank it quickly.

I said: "What did they want?" I was angry, suddenly, with the kind of anger that accompanies fear.

"It might have been worse," she said. "It wasn't really important—only unexpected. I made a fool of myself."

"How do you mean?" I asked her. Gently because of the look of horror in her eyes and the yellow, exhausted line round her mouth.

She said, almost as if she were talking to herself: "I thought it was all over and forgotten. I ought to have known that it never would be."

I said: "What did they want?" And she looked at me, blinking like someone waking from a nightmare.

"Of course it was David," she said. She sounded surprised. "They don't know about last night—I mean that we were there. They told me it was an accident. They were very kind and careful not to frighten me. Geoffrey had been to the police about David; he saw them yesterday."

"Go on," I said.

She was twisting her hands together in her lap. She looked very tired and almost frail so that a wave of protective love washed over me. She said simply:

"It's not a nice story, Tom. I suppose you have to know?"

Of course it wasn't that I had to know; rather that she had to tell me. It came out haltingly and, for Emily, in an unusually oblique fashion as if it were something that could still give her deep and immediate pain.

I had known that David had been in Belfast during the war. He was a leader-writer and working on the I.R.A. activities. He became a friend of the Hunters, having met Emily through her brother, Ruarhi, who was working with him on the same paper. They were living then in Ulster. Geoffrey was managing a shipbuilding firm and they had a house in the flat fields outside Belfast. There had been a child.

She said: "He was a nice little boy. Geoffrey was married before and his wife had died. Martin was four—a little more, perhaps, but he seemed younger, of course."

"Why should he seem younger?" I asked and she looked at me in astonishment as though I should have known.

"Oh," she said. "He was a spastic. Not a bad one, he could crawl and even talk a little. They said he would never develop very much, although he might learn to walk in time. He was a pretty child, very much like Geoffrey. We loved him dearly." She stopped.

"What happened?" I tried to take her hand but she drew away from me as if she didn't want me to touch her.

She said flatly: "I would have died rather than harm him. He was so specially dependent, you see. If he had been an ordinary child, I wouldn't have blamed myself so much. With Martin, it seemed like murder. As if I had killed him with my own hands."

At first, when she told me, it seemed that she was reading more into the thing than had ever been there. It puzzled me because she was not the sort of woman to get hysterical obsessions. Even later, when the story was developed more fully, there was still something that bewildered me as if one line of a poem was missing although the rest of it retained its sense and rhythm.

She had been playing on the lawn with the child; they had a

nannie for him, but she was on holiday in Dublin. They were sitting on a rug near to the open windows of the study and Geoffrey was working at his desk. It was high summer and thirsty weather; when David arrived and asked her to come to the hotel for a drink she was tired by the long morning and a little dazed by the sun. She had called out to Geoffrey, telling him to watch the child. It did not occur to her that he might no longer be there.

She said: "It was inexcusable. They were all very kind—they said I was thoughtless and too casual, but it was much worse than that. I knew Geoffrey had been in the study earlier. I didn't bother to look to see if he was still there or to wait until he answered me. I was in charge of Martin; I should never have left him."

She had stayed at the hotel for about twenty minutes and then David had driven her back to the house. She had known something was wrong as soon as she saw the empty rug and the toys scattered on the lawn. She had felt one moment of overwhelming panic and then it had seemed logical and inevitable that they should find his strap shoe near to the pond and the little drowned body among the water weed and the lilies.

Her eyes were dark with remembered terror and she was trembling. This time, when I tried to take her hand, she didn't draw away.

I poured her another whisky and lit her cigarette.

She said: "Of course, there was an inquest. The coroner was a friend of my father's, he was very sweet and gentle, but he had to blame me. Everyone knew about it—Northern Ireland is an awfully small world. Then Geoffrey lost his seat in the Ulster Parliament in the 1945 election. We never talked about it and I don't suppose it was really anything to do with what had happened, but I think he did blame me a little. . . ."

She looked at me sideways, squinting at me in an alarmed way. "So you can see why I was so anxious that nothing should go wrong this time."

I said: "But how could anything go wrong? And how does David come into it?" I thought I knew but I was unwilling, even though I liked him so little, to believe he could act so shabbily.

She was vague about David's part in it and a little shy, as though she were still afraid that I would be angry with her, and jealous. She had been ill after the inquest; during her illness and afterwards, David had been attentive and kind to her. He had, when I had first known him, been capable of great gentleness with people in trouble; in later years life had gone sour on him and he was gentle with no one.

For Emily he had been, at this point, a kind of saviour. He was the only person at hand to give her affection and comfort; that Geoffrey had been frighteningly distant she did not say but the implication was clear. I think to anyone else she would have told the truth; she was incapable of attacking Geoffrey to me.

She said: "He was kind, when he thought about it, but he was very busy. And I was stupidly silly and sensitive after my illness—I remember that I got upset because he was so pre-occupied with his job, though, of course, it was something he had to do. Anyway, in the end there was a certain amount of scandal about David and me, and Geoffrey didn't like it. That's why he got David sacked from his paper. David didn't know about it at the time, though I think he found out afterwards."

When they came to England and met him again he had clearly known about the harm Geoffrey had done him, and had blamed them both for it, although Emily was entirely innocent and unaware of what had happened. She had been pleased to see David and bewildered to find him so changed. His friendliness had been a very thin skin over his bitter antagonism. From his behaviour he must still have loved Emily after a fashion, but she was now more Geoffrey's wife than his own past mistress, and he hated Geoffrey.

She said: "He thought he could get his own back. The policeman told me that, at the party, he had threatened to publish the story about Martin in his gossip column, the day before the election."

I said: "If he had done that, what harm could it do?"

She looked baffled. "I don't know. A kind of smear, perhaps? An implication that Geoffrey was a bad parent?"

It was possible, I supposed, but it didn't sound good enough. I wondered if Emily had deliberately left something out, but she lied badly and she didn't look as if she were lying. And even if it were only part of the truth it was an unsavoury epitaph for David Parry.

"And the police?" I said. "What did Geoffrey tell them about David?"

"That he was blackmailing him, I think. Although it wasn't really blackmail, was it? He wasn't asking for money. I think Geoffrey thought the police could give him a fright."

"Then why did you go to see David? If Geoffrey had already been to the police?"

Her face was troubled. "He didn't tell me about the police. Or that David had mentioned Martin. Just that David had said he would put something in his paper about you and me." She hesitated and went on with apparent difficulty as though the memory was painful. Geoffrey had suggested that she should go and see Parry; she could appeal to him on the grounds of their previous closeness.

I said: "But he must have known how impossible that would be for you?"

She reddened slowly. "Why shouldn't I try to do something? After all, the mess was mostly my responsibility."

I said: "You don't have to defend Geoffrey to me. You know, don't you, that it was a swinish thing to ask you to do?"

She said defiantly: "You don't understand. I felt so at fault. I'd done Geoffrey enough harm."

I said: "You mean he told you so. But why were you responsible? Or think you were?"

She was genuinely muddled and almost tearful. She said: "I don't know. Please, Tom, let it alone."

She looked, suddenly, panic-stricken. There was no further point in questioning her; somehow we were touching on something that she still wanted to stay hidden. I said, all right, we would forget about it, and she smiled at me with weary gratitude.

It must have been about half an hour later that Geoffrey came in. We heard the front door slam and there was a lengthy, apprehensive moment before he came into the morning-room. We must both have looked startled and guilty.

He looked at the whisky bottle and then at me.

He said: "Sure you wouldn't like a room in the house old boy?"

His mouth was thin with anger. I had seen him like this before, angry in this fashion and hiding it under a layer of careful, uneasy joking. He looked tired and the whites of his eyes were bloodshot.

He sat down, picked up the whisky bottle and held it to the light.

He said: "Nice of you to leave me a drink. Will you get me a glass, dear?"

Emily poured him out a whisky, carefully not looking at me. She gave him a nervous, placating smile that drained the youth out of her face and made her look crumpled and forlorn. Earlier in the evening it had seemed ridiculous that she should pretend to be frightened of Geoffrey; now I knew that she had not been pretending. I wondered what he had done to her.

He raised his glass to her, his mouth derisive.

I said: "The police have been to see Emily. I saw them earlier to-day."

If he was surprised, he didn't show it. He raised his sandy eyebrows and grinned at me.

"What excellently reliable people they are," he said. "I take it that we are not to be arrested?"

Emily said: "They wanted to know about Martin. You didn't tell me you had been to see them, Geoffrey."

He smiled at her. "My dear, I didn't want to worry you. That business always upsets you. I couldn't have told you I was going to the police without telling you that Parry was threatening more than a scandal about you and Tom. And I had no wish to cause you pain."

He sounded genuine enough and yet there was something a little out of key. His smile was kind and yet she shrank away from him almost imperceptibly and her face was frozen. I wondered whether to remind him that he had sent Emily to the barge to see Parry, something that assorted badly with his pretended concern for her, but I wasn't sure that she had told me the truth about it.

He said: "It was just a threat. I don't really think that he would have dared to do anything—or, if he had, that it would have done me any harm. I was thinking more of the distress it would cause Emily. It would have been unpleasant for her if it had been dragged into the light after all these years." He looked at me gravely. "She has always blamed herself so much. Now you know about it, I hope that you won't blame her too."

At first I didn't think he was serious, but that it was a bad sort of joke. And then I saw that he was looking at me without any hint of laughter.

I said: "It would be absurd to think her responsible in any way."

I thought he looked a shade disappointed. As if in pleading for my understanding on Emily's behalf he had hoped himself to gain in stature, prove himself to be a good fellow, a decent chap.

Emily said: "Oh, God." She was staring at Geoffrey with complete helplessness and despair. She scrambled to her feet and went to the door. She turned, one hand on the door jamb, and said: "Thank you for coming home with me, Tom."

When she had gone, Geoffrey grinned at me wryly. "I must apologise," he said. "It was an awful business for both of us, but probably much worse for Emily. She has never quite forgiven herself—she has a very tender conscience." He grinned again. "At least, I always thought she had."

I let that one go. I said: "Why didn't you have another child? Wouldn't that have helped her?"

He regarded the tips of his long-fingered hands. "I think, that at one point, she was anxious to have a child," he said. "But it seemed to me to be a bad idea. After all, we had hardly shown ourselves to be very responsible parents, do you think?"

I felt the skin tighten round my forehead. I said: "Did you say that to Emily?" I wanted to call him a sanctimonious prig, but it was almost impossible to call Geoffrey names.

He smiled in sheer good humour and the smile lit up his face. "Hardly in so many words. It would have been bitterly unkind. I'm not quite the monster you would like to think me."

I muttered some sort of an apology and said that I must go.

Instantly he was on his feet, the good host, and asking me for my glass.

"It's a cold night," he said. "You'll have one for the road?"

He filled my glass and gave me a cigarette. There was something singularly ludicrous in his sudden care for my comfort. He settled himself back in his chair like a man preparing for a long evening, his legs stretched out to the fire and his flaxen head against a cushion. He looked handsome and scholarly; his manner was that of a university don with a private income.

Eventually he said: "You know, Tom, in another class of society I should probably have knocked your teeth in by now."

His laugh was unforced and merry, and I felt my skin prickle. I said: "I'm not sure that it wouldn't have been a healthier reaction."

"Come, come, my dear fellow," he said. "Have my gentlemanly inhibitions offended you as much as that?" He looked reflectively at his glass. "There was a murder in the town last week," he said. "A woman had been carrying on with the lodger—who was a railway man on night work—and the husband came home unexpectedly in the middle of the day and found them in bed together. He split the man's head open with a hatchet. Admirably healthy, perhaps, but wasteful. . . . Would you have preferred me to behave like that? I hardly think the poor woman, who is now left without either her husband or her lover, would agree with you."

I said: "That's an unfair argument." He paid no attention to me, but went on developing his theme with a certain amount of gusto.

"It's one way out," he said. "Murder. Or, in this case, they may commute it to manslaughter as the provocation was so extreme. They lived in one of those back-to-back houses by the gasworks; the sort of house that has a kitchen and a front parlour downstairs, two bedrooms upstairs and no bath. You manage as best you can in the kitchen sink. The husband had known about his wife and the lodger for some time. He was asked why he hadn't done anything about it—got rid of the lodger, for instance—and he said he hadn't been able to afford it. He'd been keeping a widowed mother in Bath. So they were all three shut up together, unable to get away from each other either economically or physically, mewed up in this nasty little box of a house. The woman shared her husband's bed at night and the lodger's in the daytime. The man said the housework had suffered as a result. It seemed to annoy him out of all proportion that his tea wasn't always ready when he came off work at night. One interesting thing—he said also that he couldn't have left his wife because it wouldn't have been right for her to be left alone in the house with a man she wasn't married to. He was apparently quite serious about it. Now you and I, Tom"—he smiled expansively—"aren't concerned about our respectability, we don't have to live together. And we can talk about it, work it out of our systems, in a way that poor devil sitting in prison presumably couldn't do. So the thing doesn't build itself up into violence . . . it wouldn't give either of us any relief. It would just leave a nasty taste in the mouth."

I was surprised to find he had so much imagination.

I said: "Is this some sort of apologia? Or a thesis to prove that crimes of passion don't happen in the middle class?"

He wasn't smiling now. "Neither," he said. "Perhaps an apology for myself. At bottom, however educated or civilised we may be, don't we all have an uneasy feeling that it would be more proper to react to this sort of nonsense like a caveman with his club? I imagine, anyway, that it is how you feel. You are more straightforward than I am, Tom. I don't feel like that at all. I liked you before this happened and I like you still. Can you understand that?"

I wondered if he meant it. He stroked the fair hair back from his forehead with a weary gesture and looked at me in a puzzled way as if there really were something that he didn't properly understand and would like to have explained to him. He seemed more vulnerable than I had ever seen him, and I wasn't angry any longer, only sorry.

I said: "I'm not sure that I do understand. And does it do any good to talk? It gets us no nearer a solution."

He sounded worried. "Doesn't it? I'm not sure that I agree with

97

you. I should have thought that it helped to clarify, to put things into perspective."

He smiled, this time almost anxiously, and I was suddenly aware that he was trying to be friendly with me. I felt instantly and unreasonably wary.

He went on: "After all, Tom, our interests are the same in this. You know Emily well, though perhaps not as well as I know her. She's a nice, sweet, good-hearted creature, but completely at the mercy of her own emotions. If we're not sensible, you and I, she'll get us both into the kind of mess that would suit neither of us."

I said: "What do you expect me to do?" Waiting for the sharpness of the steel beneath the velvet.

It was there all right. "Stop seeing her," he said. "At least for a while. Don't come to the house. Don't talk to her on the telephone. She'll get over it—and though I don't expect you to believe me now, so will you. These things don't last, although they may seem important at the time. And we both have so much to lose."

He was pompous and unbearably smug. He looked so safe and so confident, sitting at ease in his well-upholstered chair, wearing an excellently-cut suit and hand-made shoes.

I said: "What else did you tell the police? When you went to see them about David?"

He scratched his head and looked rueful like a small boy caught out in a lie which he confidently expects the grownups to find funny.

He said: "You're clever, Tom, aren't you?"

I said sharply: "Gutter-brightness. I've had to be or I would have ended up as an errand boy."

He knocked out his pipe on the sole of his shoe and filled it slowly. When it was alight he looked at me steadily and said: "I told them that David was threatening me on two counts. Because of the circumstances of my son's death and because of Emily's behaviour with you. I fancy that the second thing was the most important and the one he could have done most damage with. And easier to hint at in a gossip column without running the risk of libel."

"I see." I could feel the jumping muscle in my cheek and the room seemed suddenly very small and hot. "So their visit to me this afternoon may not have been entirely because David was my brother-in-law? Because I might reasonably be expected to have had a fight with him and knocked him down?"

He said solemnly: "I'm afraid that may be true, Tom. Believe me, I'm sorry. But you must remember that I had no idea, when I went to the police, what was going to happen later in the day."

"This hurts you more than it hurts me," I said, and got up from my chair. He was with me before I reached the door, his face anxious and contrite.

"I would far rather not have had to tell them about you and Emily," he said.

I think, at that moment, he honestly believed he was speaking the truth. Perhaps he, even believed it to be true that he liked me and bore me no ill-will. I wondered how he managed to deceive himself so completely; it was a nice talent and must have made his life a more comfortable one than most.

I caught that last bus back to the town, got off at the terminus and walked the last, cold mile. The sky was wintry and high and flecked with October stars.

The house was dark; I stumbled over Sandy's satchel in the hall and cracked my head on the banister rail.

A camp-bed had been set up for me in the sitting-room; my pyjamas and dressing-gown were laid on a chair beside it. I felt faintly embarrassed and wondered whether Nora had locked the bedroom door.

It was an old camp-bed and rocky. There weren't enough blankets and my feet were cold. After a long while I went to sleep.

I woke up suddenly; the light was on and Nora was kneeling beside me. She was huddled in an old coat and the tears were pouring down her face. She wasn't touching me, but I had the impression that she had been trying to wake me.

I said: "What on earth are you doing here? Go back to bed. You'll make yourself ill."

She was shuddering and shaking, her face was swollen and her hair was tangled and looked dull. I sat up with an effort and put my arm round her.

She wriggled away half-heartedly, making her point as it were, but remaining within the circle of my arm.

She said: "Don't. You don't want to touch me, do you? I must look awful. I couldn't sleep, I was waiting for you to come in. Tom, I'm so miserable."

I rocked her in my arms, feeling the intolerable burden of my responsibility.

In the end, she said: "Tom, come upstairs to bed. It's terribly cold down here."

Chapter Eight

The inspector arrived just after I had finished the last of my morning tutorials. Since the moment of waking I had spent the hours in chilling expectation of disaster, so that when he finally appeared, ordinary and tired and badly dressed, fear took on a human shape and was no longer nameless.

His name was Walker. He stood in the high old room, as ill-at-ease as any penniless undergraduate in his first term, regarding the lines of books with an air of cautious reverence.

He said: "Nice place you have here, Mr. Harrington."

He had not brought the sergeant with him; he sat, shabby and alone, in the chair where my pupils normally sat, and as uneasily upright. His small feet were planted neatly together on the carpet before him, and the outline of his bony knees was visible beneath the thin tweed of his trousers. I felt confidence flow back into me; I was on my home ground now, and I had been prepared for him.

He said: "Mr. Harrington, I believe you had a quarrel with your brother-in-law? About someone you were friendly with?"

I said: "Hardly a quarrel. He told me that he knew. But you have already been told about it, haven't you?"

"It has been brought to our notice. You were concerned, I imagine, that your wife should remain unaware of this—friendship?"

His delicacy was absurd. He seemed, himself, to be nervously aware of its absurdity. He looked at me in a manner that was unhappy and shy.

I said: "When I met him in the Woolpack, he told me that he knew about my *affaire* with Mrs. Hunter. He said that he had no intention of telling my wife and apart from trying to borrow five pounds from me on the strength of it, nothing more was said. There was certainly no quarrel."

"I see." He gave a small sigh of relief as though he felt that the awkwardly disagreeable preliminaries were over. "I understand, however, that he informed Mr. Hunter of the situation between you and his wife? That must have been unpleasant for you."

"I knew nothing of it until last night," I said.

He went on: "Mr. Parry had been a friend of Mrs. Hunter's. Had he told you that? It must have made difficulties between you."

I said flatly: "We did not quarrel. My brother-in-law was a malicious man. He liked to make trouble; I knew that and so I wouldn't allow myself to get angry. We weren't good friends, but we weren't enemies either."

He nodded and looked out of the window at the grey quadrangle and the moving sky. I wondered how old he was. His skin was dry and flaky and wrinkled round the eyes from smiling; ten years ago he had probably looked as he did now and it was improbable that the next ten years would see much change in him. He was that kind of man.

He said abstractedly, as if it were not of any great importance: "You are quite sure that you did not see Mr. Parry, on his barge, last night?"

He turned his gaze from the window and towards me and his eyes were suddenly bright and lively with interest.

He was gently apologetic. "You must understand that this is not official. Only sometimes people withhold things mistakenly. It isn't only the guilty who lie; even the innocent are often afraid that their actions may be misinterpreted. The police are not as stupid as they are occasionally thought to be."

He no longer looked insignificant. He was sharp and alert, and smiling a little. I met his brown eyes and hoped I looked sure of myself.

My mouth seemed to move in a stiff and jerky fashion.

I said: "I have not lied to the police, now or at any other time."

It seemed that I was being given endless chances of redemption; I saw myself throwing them away with terrifying inevitability.

He looked immediately saddened, and I felt guilty in the way that a child feels when he has been expected to own up by his schoolmaster and failed to do so. His silence was somehow a reproach.

I went on: "Did you think I had lied?"

He looked shocked as if I had said something improper.

"Oh, no," he said. "It wasn't an accusation, you know." And then, with the air of a man leaving a painful subject: "We had the report of the post-mortem, this morning."

I wondered whether it was in keeping with innocence to ask the obvious question; he seemed to expect me to do so.

"What was the result?" I said.

He opened his hands and held them palm upwards in a quietly despairing gesture.

"Indefinite, sir," he said. "Not that there is ever anything very clear cut in these cases, but we had hoped for something a little more helpful. Your brother-in-law died from a cranial injury, Mr. Harrington. There was a fracture of the skull and extensive damage to the brain. There had been a haemorrhage of the middle meningeal artery."

His voice was careful, as if he were speaking some unfamiliar tongue.

I had no idea what he meant. I said slowly: "How do you think it happened?" I moved my body in the chair and felt my clothes damp with sweat and clinging to me.

He shrugged his shoulders. "How can we tell? He wasn't drunk, and it was a violent fall for a man who had done no more than stumble. I am told, that with this kind of injury, a man falling will concuss himself. Then, if it is serious, the concussion will pass into symptoms of compressison of the brain. The surgeon tells me that it is possible that there would be what he called a 'lucid interval' between the concussion and the final coma."

I hoped I didn't sound too eager. "Then if he fell inside the barge, he might have gone outside to get help? And then collapsed again?"

I tried not to think of David opening the cabin door on to the wind and the night, and the beating rain. I wondered if he had called for help before he fell on to the slippery boards of the gangplank and died there.

He was looking at his hands. "It might have happened like that," he said. "They can't tell." He went on almost lightly, as if death were not a very important matter. "The river finished him, of course. There was water in the lungs. But we would like to know more about the original injury."

I said: "It must be unsatisfactory for you."

His eyes were tired and shrewd. "Very," he said. "These things so often are. Especially as in this case I am told it is rather unlikely that he would have had a lucid interval. I don't pretend to understand the mechanics of it, but it is something to the effect that the meningeal artery connects directly with the brain which means that the damage is more immediate and serious. Oh—no one will say anything definite. There's nothing as cagey as a pathologist."

He sighed, stared at me for a moment, and then got to his feet. He returned to his earlier, uncertain manner. He looked gauche and shy, and out of place.

"I'm sorry to have troubled you again," he said. Then, hesitantly: "This car. The one that knocked you down. You are quite sure you can't help us there?"

I shook my head. "It was a shock, you see. The car was being driven very fast and it was dark."

"Unfortunate." He sounded thoughtful. "No one in that area had a visitor last night who came by car. We would very much like to know who was driving it and where it was going. I expect you know, sir, the lane is a dead end."

I said: "Perhaps someone took the wrong road?"

His face brightened as if I had said something original and helpful. "That's quite possible. But if that were so it's difficult to see why the car didn't stop when it hit you, or, indeed, why it was going so fast that it couldn't brake, in time. If the driver had been unsure of the road, wouldn't he have been going more slowly?"

He looked at me with an air of reserve and I was conscious of the small, hard core of authority beneath the diffident politeness.

He said: "Perhaps Mr. Parry had a visitor last night after all.

Try and remember about the car, Mr. Harrington. It might help both of us."

The words were too gently spoken to be a threat. He smiled as he said good-bye, and shook my hand.

Mrs. Parry said: "She's gone out to lunch with Mr. Hunter."

Her movements, as she laid the table, were heavy and tired; the skin was flaccid round her jaw bone. She seemed, in the course of a night, to have acquired the pathos and defencelessness of age. The flesh, had loosened on her face and the big nose stood out like a bridge, her pale eyes sunken on either side of it.

Geoffrey had telephoned at noon and called for Nora half an hour later. She had been excited and pleased; she had worn her new suit and her best hat.

Mrs. Parry said sourly: "What's sauce for the goose is sauce for the gander."

I said: "What the hell do you mean?" And she looked at me with an air of obscene triumph and said: "Well, you don't think you're the only one who can play this sort of game, do you? Do you expect them not to try to get a bit of their own back?"

I said: "There is nothing so thoroughly nasty as the mind of a good woman."

It went over her head; she went on, with the same kind of revengeful pleasure.

"You'll make a nice mess for yourselves, the four of you. But you'll have to pay for it in the end, mark my words. And it won't be pleasant. Wicked and selfish—that's what you all are. Greedy—never a decent thought for others. My son is dead and my only daughter doesn't think of me and what I may be suffering. Oh, no. She's off out with the first man who asks her. Sex—that's the only thing you ever think of. Just like a lot of nasty animals. . . ."

There was a lot more and it was all revolting. It was like lifting the lid of a long-buried coffin and it made me sick with horror. I stayed as long as I could because she was an unhappy woman and she was old and tired, but in the end I couldn't stand it any longer.

I left the table and my unfinished lunch and went out of the house, half-running down the road. Running away from the sparkle of venonz in her pale eyes and her unclean tongue. I remember that I looked continuously over my shoulder as if I were afraid she would follow me.

My heart was pounding when I reached the river, and not from physical exertion. I sat by the brown water, on a pile of crackling leaves, and smoked one cigarette after another. I felt dirty, as if I had been touched by something far worse than ordinary human wickedness and failure.

Then the feeling of contamination went and I felt, as always, that I had behaved badly. I should have stayed and let her work it out of her system; it was cowardly and cruel to leave her. She had looked ill, she had genuine cause for grievance and I should have tried to help her. Then even that seemed presumptuous and I was back again in the familiar circle of guilt and self-recrimination. I wondered whether everyone felt like this and so continuously.

Geoffrey, I thought, was not the kind. Doubt never troubled him, nor any sense of failure. He was armoured with success.

I felt hatred crawl in my stomach until my limbs were trembling and I was sick with it. It was something I had come to live with. Until the last few days it had walked beside me obscurely, like a shadow; now it had acquired form and substance and could no longer be ignored.

Nora said: "Geoffrey says I would be silly to divorce you."

She had arrived in my rooms in college in the middle of the afternoon. She was pink and giggly and still a little tipsy from lunch; the make-up had gone greasy on her face and her eyes were hard and shiny with drink. She was wearing very high-heeled shoes and an unsuitably fussy hat. Her manner was a mixture of shyness and excitement; she kicked off her shoes as if they hurt her and curled up in the armchair; talking in a machine-gun fashion like a child who has been taken for an unexpected treat. She told me where she had been and what she had to eat, how kind Geoffrey had been to her and how understanding. It had been a successful lunch; he had found, for Nora, the right kind of flattery. He had told her that she had a good, clear, trained mind and should be doing something more important than looking after a home and a husband. She repeated this, staring at me with bright defiance. Then she said, with an air almost of archness, her little piece about divorce.

I knew that it was her only weapon and that she was using it as such; nevertheless, the words, once spoken in her light clipped voice, were irretrievable. In the startled silence that followed them she seemed to crumple, the ebullient mood left her and she picked nervously at the stuff of her skirt.

I said: "Were you thinking of doing so?"

She gave me a tight, artificial smile. "No. Not really," she said. Her voice was frightened and uncertain as if she had said something she had not meant to say. She went on, unhappily: "Of course I'd thought of it. What did you expect? And I told Geoffrey so." She said his Christian name a little coyly. "But it was only an impulse. I think—and he agrees with me—that it would be foolish. After all, Emily is a wildly emotional sort of person—almost adolescent in a way. She's not educated, or even particularly intelligent and these things do count, don't they? I mean, you haven't had to live with her. I dare say this sort of love affair is exciting and I expect she's good in bed, but it isn't the whole of life, is it? After all, being married to someone and living with them all the time is a different thing from just being in love with them. The everyday things are more important. I expect you *do* think you are in love with her—but this kind of love is the sort of thing you read about in penny magazines. It doesn't happen in real life, not among grown people."

If the echo of Geoffrey's voice hadn't been so clear, it might have been funny. As it was, she sounded like a child repeating, without understanding, the words of an adult, and it saddened me.

I said: "Nora, do you really think like that?"

She flushed with annoyance and bit her lip. Then she said, angrily: "Of course I do. If you had really loved her, you would have taken her away when she asked you to."

I said: "I suppose Geoffrey told you that?"

It was useless to say to her that it wasn't so simple; it was no good trying to explain at all.

She began to cry in a slow, hiccuping sort of way. "Oh, Tom," she said, "don't you see what a dreadful thing you have done to me? Why did you do it? You must have hated me so much."

I wondered if she would always see what had happened as a deep, personal affront.

I said: "Dear, I don't hate you. You must know that. It isn't like that at all."

She didn't take any notice. She went on crying in a persistent, drunken fashion until she began to yawn a little, rubbing her hot eyes with the back of her hand and tipping the silly hat sideways on her head.

She said: "Tom, I'm so tired. Can I go to sleep here?"

I thought of Mrs. Parry, alone in the empty house.

I said: "Hadn't you better go home to your mother?"

It seemed, suddenly, that between us we were forgetting the thing that had overshadowed our private unhappiness; I looked at Nora and felt ashamed and petty. But she stared blankly at me as if she didn't understand what I was saying, and I knew that, to her, David's death had become relatively unimportant.

I said: "I'll get a taxi and take you home. You can sleep there."

She gave me a sleepy grateful smile. I rang through to the lodge and asked them to get me a taxi. I gave her a towel and told her to go and wash her face. She came back from the bathroom with the make-up washed off her face and her hat in her hand. She had combed her hair loosely round her face and she looked tired and young.

When we got home, the house was empty; Mrs. Parry had left a note saying she had gone out to do the shopping. I took Nora upstairs to bed. She stood quite still while I undressed her and turned back the covers. I tidied up her clothes and hung her suit up in the wardrobe. She watched me from the bed. When I had finished she stretched out an arm; I went and sat on the bed beside her and held her hand.

I said: "Go to sleep now. You'll feel much better after an hour or two. It's silly to drink too much at lunchtime."

Her forehead creased as if she were trying to remember something. Then she said:

"Tom, you didn't tell me that you were out with Emily on the night that David was killed."

She said it quite naturally as if it were not at all important, merely something that I had omitted to tell her. It was an effort to remember that she knew nothing at all about the way that David had died.

I said carefully: "Who told you?"

She yawned and snuggled down under the covers.

"Geoffrey said so. He said you were silly not to tell the police yourself because they were bound to find out." She looked at me slyly, through half-closed eyes. "Tom, where did you go, you and Emily? When you were together, I mean?"

It seemed somehow indecent that she should ask me that. I remember that I was not only embarrassed but quite extraordinarily shocked by her prurient curiosity.

I said: "We weren't together all that much. Don't torment yourself about it. What else did Geoffrey tell you?"

She said sleepily: "Oh, nothing much. Just that Emily had gone to pick you up from the Fosters' and knocked you off your bicycle. He said you hadn't told the police about it—although I don't know why that matters—and that it was awkward, because someone saw the car down the lane and they had been making inquiries at the garage. Is it important, Tom? I'm so dreadfully tired."

"No," I said. "It isn't important. Try and sleep."

I stayed with her until she was breathing heavily; when she was finally asleep her mouth opened a little and the grip of her hot hand relaxed.

Then I went downstairs and rang Geoffrey. There was no answer. I rang at regular intervals throughout the evening and there was still no reply.

Chapter Nine

Emily had been making apple jam. I sat on the kitchen table and watched her as she covered the jars with circles of white waxed paper, and tied them round with string. She wrote the month and the year on small labels and stuck them on the sides of the jars. She was deft and methodical where Nora would have been clumsy; her hands, which were big and strong-fingered for a woman, were quick and competent.

She said: "I don't know why he told them. There was no need. . . ."

Her eyes were unhappy and darkly circled; the whites were unclear and her skin looked muddy. Her shoulders sagged a little as though from a weight of tiredness. When she had finished sticking on the labels, she took the jars, two at a time, one in each hand and stacked them in rows in the store cupboard.

She straightened her back wearily and pushed the soft hair away from, her forehead with a gesture that she had borrowed from Geoffrey.

She said: "He thought that it seemed simpler to tell them a little of the truth. They were already curious—it was better to appear to be open with them."

The police had been waiting for Geoffrey when he came home after his lunch with Nora. He had been shut in his study with Walker for more than an hour. Emily had waited in the hall, wondering and fearful, unable to hear what they were saying and unwilling to move, ready to hide in the kitchen if the door should open.

I knew how Geoffrey would look to Walker as if I had been in the room with him. He would have made an excellent impression, sitting at ease in his leather chair, his light eyes wide and honest. He would have appeared to Walker as he would have appeared to anyone: a decent chap making a clean breast of a difficult and distasteful story. And it would have fitted in better with the picture he was presenting to say that his wife and her lover had lied for the old and obvious reason than to have no story to tell at all.

I said: "Maybe he's right. Maybe it is easier this way. If the wolves are coming, you chuck out the weakest and keep them occupied for a while."

She said uncertainly: "Geoffrey thinks it will be all right. He said it might protect us all."

I said: "That's kind of him. So the story runs that you came to meet me at the Fosters'. That you had arranged to meet me there and that, inadvertently, you ran me down. Naturally we lied, you and I, because we didn't want anyone to know about our little *affaire*. But Geoffrey already knew, didn't he? And the police know that he knew. How did he explain that away?"

Her voice was spent. "We might have said that we wouldn't meet again. It would be enough if only I had promised not to see you. Then it would still be reasonable to lie, wouldn't it?"

I said: "Would we have lied in a thing like this? When David was dead, and our movements had to be accounted for?"

She put her hand to her mouth and stared at me with eyes, that were blue and fearful.

She said: "But, Tom, if we knew nothing about that—if we were innocent and had nothing to be afraid of, surely, then, it wouldn't matter to us what the police thought? It would only matter that Geoffrey and Nora shouldn't know we had been together."

I said: "I suppose so. But what about the other car? If they've been to the garage, they must know that Geoffrey took it out that night."

Everything seemed to be very far away but clear, like distant mountains seen on a bright, still day.

She said softly: "He had some letters—important letters—to take to the general post office in the town. The last collection had already gone from the village. That was what he said to the man at the garage when he went to fetch the car. There is no reason why they should not believe him now."

I said: "He thinks ahead, doesn't he? But why the hell did he have to tell them about you and me? Was he scared?"

She smiled as she might have smiled at a child's absurdity. "Oh, no. He wasn't scared. He never is. He is so sure."

I said: "I don't get it. If he was so sure and so safe on his pinnacle, and not at all afraid, then why give so much of the game away?"

Her mouth quivered a little. "Just because he is sure. He knows that he is in command and that nothing can ever touch him. It makes him overreach himself, always."

She stopped and looked self-conscious as if she had said more than she had meant to say. I asked her what she was talking about, but she shook her head and, her eyes had a frightened, abstracted look as if she knew that what she had said was true, but did not know why. She was good at emotional, intuitive judgments although I had always thought her blind about Geoffrey. Now, suddenly, I wondered whether it might not have been a protective measure for herself.

I asked her where I could find Geoffrey and she said he was in the workshop cleaning his guns.

"I hope Nora found him a comfort yesterday," she said. She gave me a shadow of a smile. "I found her ear-rings in the car They had slipped down between the two front seats."

We both laughed a little and then I kissed her. She was soft and warm and her breath smelt of jam. In my arms she relaxed a little, her eyes big and shining as if she were near to tears.

I said: "Emily, why haven't you left him before?"

It was the first time I had ever asked her that. I think I had been too afraid that she loved him. I know that I had always thought he was necessary to her.

She frowned a little and said, surprisingly: "Because he thinks so clearly." Her voice was uncertain as if she were out of her depth. If I had asked Nora a similar question in like circumstances she would have answered immediately and it would have sounded plausible. Emily was too honest to be glib; now, she pulled herself away from me and her eyes were afraid and her mouth small and taut.

"I can't really explain. It's something to do with his always being so right and making other people seem so muddled. He is clever, you know, and living with him you get so that it's easier to accept what he says is true than work it out for yourself. He doesn't want me to leave him, and if I had done so for my own reasons I should have felt terribly in the wrong. I've often *felt* that something was right and not been able to explain why; with Geoffrey, the explanation is always more important than the feeling so he is able to twist you round to his way of thinking and you believe he must be right."

She looked at me in a shy and puzzled way.

She said: "Tom, you're the only person I've ever met who's more muddled than I am, and yet it doesn't seem to matter with you. You're half-conventional, half-religious, if you like, and in a funny sort of way you're more right than Geoffrey who's never been half-anything in his life."

Her face was hot with the effort to explain. She caught hold of my arms and shook me gently. I think I did understand, dimly, what she was trying to say, but just then I was more grateful for her belief in me and her obvious love than for her stumbling judgment. I kissed her again and held her tightly. And then I went to look for Geoffrey.

He was wearing a Harris tweed sports coat patched with leather at the elbows, a canary-yellow pullover, breeches and boots. It was hot in the workshop and there was a smell of leather and oil. He had a pair of twelve-bore double-barrelled guns on the table one still in its mahogany box and the other in his hands. He was rubbing down the barrel and the silver chasing on the butt was clear and polished. Outside the autumn sun was bright; it fell through the narrow, cobwebbed window and glinted on the eddying dust and on the shining guns and on Geoffrey's flaxen head.

He looked up as I came in and his smile was cautious. The colour deepened under the thin, fair skin.

He said: "Hallo, old chap. You're early this morning."

The shaft was blunt. I told him that I had been talking to Emily. I told him that I knew he had seen the police.

He broke the gun and peered intently down the barrel. His mouth was wry.

"Annoyed with me?" he said.

The back of his head was thin and pointed; his neck, where the fair hair grew clipped and low almost to the collar of his jacket, was bent and vulnerable. I felt my hands stiffen and clench, and thrust them deep into my trouser pockets.

My mouth was dry. I said: "What do you expect me to do? Congratulate you?"

His eyes were the washed-out blue of a spring sky. There were thin threads of scarlet in the corners. He looked anxious.

He said uneasily: "Don't lose your temper, Tom. It was the only thing to do. I wasn't deliberately involving you. We're all in this together."

"Some of us appear to be more deeply in than others," I said.

He gave me a startled look and stood up. He took the other gun out of the mahogany box and handed it to me.

"Let's get out of here," he said.

I felt clumsy with the gun; it was a long time since I had been shooting and I had almost forgotten how to carry it. We walked out of the workshop into the garden and through the small gate at the end that led to the fields behind the house. We climbed, on the sloping turf, to the patch of woodland on the top of the low hill; there were mare's tails in the sky and a wet, gentle wind blowing. In the neighbouring fields, hens scratched among the corn stubble and the air was filled with the broken hum of tractors. We stopped at the stile at the entrance to the wood and Geoffrey leaned on one knee crinkled his eyes across the valley, and said, to the manner born.

"Jenkins has got a decent herd of Red Polls there."

He looked and sounded like a gentleman farmer; it was not a

pose and was as genuine as Geoffrey the politician, Geoffrey the scholar. I was wearing a dark suit, a white shirt and black shoes, and felt as out of place as an insurance clerk.

Then Geoffrey explained about Walker. The confidence had returned to his voice and he no longer looked anxious. I felt as if somehow I had lost the initiative without realising that I had ever had it.

Walker had been waiting for him at the house; he was sitting in the study with a cup of coffee balanced awkwardly on his knee. He had been polite but dogged and his interest had become clear. He had already inquired about Geoffrey's car; he had learned from the garage that it was being resprayed and that it had been badly scratched. He had appeared to accept Geoffrey's assurance that the spraying was merely routine, but he had come back to it again and again with courteous tenacity. In the end he had mentioned my accident with the bicycle.

Geoffrey said: "After that I had to tell him. I did my best to sound pretty casual. I said that my wife had had the car out the night before, that I hadn't noticed any scratches on the wing, but that I wasn't in the habit of looking for them. I let him drag the rest of the story out of me—it seemed to be the most convincing way to handle it as I hadn't told the truth in the beginning. In the end I told him that she'd said she'd gone to meet you, but hadn't mentioned anything about an accident. I gave him to understand that I was pretty fussy about the Bentley and that Emily would have preferred, whatever the circumstances, not to tell me she had damaged it. Naturally, I explained that neither of you would have been particularly anxious to tell the police what had happened. It wouldn't have seemed necessary and nobody likes to wash their dirty linen in front of strangers—not even the police. I said that I had myself hoped to be able to respect my wife's confidence or I would have been more honest with him in the beginning. He quite understood and he said he hoped it wouldn't have to go any further. . . ."

It struck me, then, that he wasn't in the least concerned with the moral implications; that to him, keeping out of trouble in a murder case was no more important than a customs evasion.

I said: "You made a nice smoke screen for yourself, didn't you?"

His laughter was simple and unaffected. He slapped his breeches with his free hand and his eyes were amused and kindly.

"Don't be an idiot, Tom," he said. "No harm's done. The man has no real reason to be suspicious of any of us—he was only being officious. He's probably due for promotion or something. Now he knows that we were all hiding something that it was, in fact, quite reasonable to hide, it's not likely that he'll risk making a fool of himself by looking any farther."

"All right," I said. "And so you've thrown him off the scent. What am I supposed to do about it?"

The laughter died on his thin mouth and he looked suitably grave.

"Go along and see him," he said. "Tell him you've thought it over and decided to tell the truth. The police aren't, after all, guardians of public morals. There's no need for you to be embarrassed."

I said: "It was muddy down the lane. Won't there have been tracks? And if there were tracks they would have found the marks of two cars, not one."

He shrugged his shoulders. "It's a risk," he said. "But not, I think, a serious one. If they have any suspicions about Parry's death it's probably to our advantage if they think another car went down the lane that night. Honestly, Tom, I don't think you should worry any more."

His face was clear and untroubled in the sun. He vaulted the stile and grinned at me.

"You mustn't confuse your own feelings of guilt and responsibility with fear of the police," he said.

After that, we were silent for a while. We got a brace of partridge, about half a dozen wood pigeon and a couple of rabbits. I was ridiculously pleased to find I was a better shot than I had expected to be, and that Geoffrey was surprisingly bad. Both the partridges were mine and most of the pigeon.

In the end we came to a clearing in the centre of the wood and the edge of a Roman camp. There had been a digging there some years before; now the grass had grown smooth over it and it looked like a natural hollow. In the grassy bottom some boys had made a hideout and abandoned it. There were the charred remains of a fire and a few, rusty saucepans.

The wind had changed and it was gusty and suddenly cold although the sun was bright.

Geoffrey said: "I've got some coffee. Let's get down there, out of the cold."

He looked frozen. His face was pinched and mauve round the lips and his skin was pimpled with cold. I started down the slope. It was comparatively steep and once out of the wind the chill went from the air, and the sun was warm on the back of my neck.

Then I saw Geoffrey's shadow. It was thrown long by the sun and stretched in front of me. His gun was raised at his shoulder and pointed at my back.

I felt a sick lurch of fear and then, curiously, calmness. I remembered his story about the railway worker and his wife's lover. I thought how easily explained a shooting accident would be. I felt a kind of wonder that he should think me worth killing and knew that I had always believed he considered me of very little importance. I think that, in the midst of fear, I was almost proud.

Of course I turned round. And Geoffrey was standing where I had left him at the top of the bluff, his gun loose at his side, looking at the sky. I wheeled round to face down the slope again and saw his tall figure with the menacing, pointed gun, and remembered that the sun plays odd tricks with shadows.

I think I laughed out loud. I know that suddenly Geoffrey was looking at me curiously, as if there were something about me that surprised him, before he started down the slope towards me.

We sat side by side, our backs against the curving side of the hollow, and drank the hot, sweet coffee, taking turns with the Thermos cup.

He said: "You know, Tom, I think I managed to talk Nora out of divorcing you."

I wondered whether I was expected to thank him.

"I think it was pretty unlikely, anyway," I said.

He looked at me sideways. "Do you? I'm glad of that." Then he grinned at me as if I were one of the boys. "I think, between you and me, that she was almost enjoying herself and her feeling of being the wronged little wife."

I said: "It's a comparatively strong position, haven't you found it so?"

His face became solemn and his voice, avuncular.

He said: "We should respect her feelings, I think. It is too easy to be frivolous about this sort of thing. And rather regrettable. It is obvious that she loves you, Tom. You didn't expect her not to be hurt and angry, did you? It is natural for her to feel deeply insulted, but I should think that if you played your cards carefully you should be able to get her back. After all, you have been married for eight years. It's not a thing to be lightly discarded."

I said: "Thanks for the advice." I got up and took my gun and climbed up out of the hollow. I walked through the wood, kicking at the carpet of leaves, until I came to the far side of the wood. The sky was clouding over and the sun had gone from, my side of the valley, but over on the far hill it lit a field of late, uncut corn, rippling it with waves of gold and darker gold until, it had the colour and texture of a Chinese carpet.

I fired a dozen cartridges at a young, sapling birch at the end of the field and the delicate trunk shivered with each shot. Then I walked back through the wood to the Roman working.

Geoffrey was sitting where I had left him, his head tilted back against the turf. The gun lay on the ground at his side and his hands were loose on his knees. He was fast asleep.

I went quietly down, suddenly quite aware of what I was going to do. It had all been made so simple for me. I could be expected to be unhandy with a gun. I had no reason to kill Geoffrey, or no reason that would mean very much to a policeman or in a court of law. There are always shooting accidents. There would be people who would think that Geoffrey had brought it on himself by putting a gun in the hands of someone so unused to handling it.

I went up to him. His head had fallen a little on one side and the tendons of his neck were standing out like wires beneath the flesh. His mouth was slightly open and his breath whistled as though his position were uncomfortable. His hair had been blown untidy by the wind and stood up at the back in absurd, spiky tufts like a schoolboy's. His hands were blue-veined and looked cold; otherwise, he was sleeping very neatly, with his knees drawn up towards his chest and his hands resting lightly on them. In sleep his face looked tired and scholarly.

I thought: I will have to shoot him from a distance because it will look less suspicious. I wonder how far away it will have to be if it is going to look like an accident. I will have to kill him at the first shot, otherwise he will wake.

For a moment, the terror of missing him and having him wake and see me standing there, went through me and made me sick. Then I walked away from him, walking carefully backwards and on my toes, although the grass was soft and soundless, and he was sleeping very deeply.

I thought that if I stood on the edge of the working and shot him from there, I could say that I had aimed at a rabbit on the far side of the hollow and caught my foot in a hole and stumbled. There were plenty of rabbits; the clearing was full of warrens and grey pellet droppings.

Then I realised that it would be better to shoot him somewhere among the trees, in the thickest part of the wood, where I could say I hadn't seen him. I wondered if there would be much blood on the green cropped grass, and if it would be safe to carry him home and say he had died elsewhere.

He stirred in his sleep and stretched out one of his legs slowly, as if it were cramped. His hand fell limply away from its support and lay open on the ground.

I don't know at what point I knew it was useless. I tried to tell myself afterwards that it was his helplessness, his look of ordinary humanity that stopped me. But it wasn't true. It was my own weakness and my own bungling and failure.

When I knew I couldn't do it, I began to run away from the

camp. I ran fast, stumbling among the blackberry bushes that grew thick and tangled and low. At last my foot caught in a briar and I fell, cracking my chin on the butt of the gun. I lay among the bushes, my scratched hands covering my face and the warm blood running into my mouth and cried and cried like an adolescent until I was tired and soggy and weak. And then I got up and wiped my mouth and my hands, and went back to fetch Geoffrey.

Chapter Ten

The pain started in the bus on the way to the police station. I had been aware of it for some time but only as a vague and irritating discomfort, a solid lump of pain that seemed to be located behind my diaphragm. My mouth tasted foul; I lit a cigarette and the smoke was harsh and sour against my tongue. I shifted my position on the seat and huddled forward, wrapping my arms round my body. The woman beside me looked at me curiously and edged a little away.

The bus stopped and I got up cautiously; the pain was no worse when I stood upright. By the time I had got off the bus and was walking along the pavement, I had discovered that I was able to live with it. It had become an accepted part of me; I discovered that if I held my stomach muscles in a certain way it was more bearable.

When I got to the police station they said I would have to wait; Inspector Walker was busy. I sat on a wooden seat in a long, bare corridor, wondering how soon I would be able to get to a doctor. The physical discomfort had momentarily removed my apprehension so that when I was shown into Walker's room I was not at all dismayed and only anxious to get the whole thing over as quickly as possible.

Walker was alone, small and shabby behind a bland and polished desk. The room was obsessionally neat, there was no clutter, no untidy files. On the leather surface of the desk a pair of Georgian inkwells, proudly polished, flanked a silver pen tray, and all the time I was talking Walker played with a penknife with a beautifully-carved handle. He ran his slender fingers up and down the blunt blade; when I stumbled finally into silence he laid the knife neatly in the exact centre of the blotter in front of him and looked, not at me but at the painted wall behind my shoulder.

I was suddenly afraid. The story had sounded lame and foolish and because it was not entirely true I felt its falseness must be immediately clear and apparent to the silent little man behind the desk.

In the end, he looked at me and smiled. It was a glowing smile, curiously sweet, although his eyes looked tired and sore at the edges as though he had been rubbing them.

He said: "I'm glad you came, Mr. Harrington."

The flatness of his midland voice was somehow incongruous beside the civilised beauty of his possessions. It was an uncultured voice, the voice of a man who made no attempt to conceal his origins.

He picked up the paper-knife again and fiddled with it nervously as if the interview were not to his liking. The smile had left, his face and without it he looked dry and middle-aged and weary.

He said: "It had worried us, you know. Your accident with the bicycle, I mean. You'd had a nasty knock—you might have been killed. Frankly, I didn't understand why you were so little concerned with finding the car that had knocked you down. It wasn't natural now, was it? After all, the owner of the car would have had to pay for the repairs to your bicycle. Of course we had nothing to go on—it was only by chance that we found out about Mr. Hunter's Bentley and that Mrs. Hunter had been driving it. The mechanic at the garage told us that the left wing had been badly scratched. Then of course things began to fall into place. . . ."

I wondered why he was being so open with me and what chance had taken him to the garage. It sounded a far-fetched piece of luck and he didn't look clever or particularly percipient, just ordinary, conscientious and rather dull. There was no surprise in his voice or condemnation; he sounded like a man who had lived for so long with falsehood and petty wickedness that he no longer found it unexpected.

He said: "I suppose you have already seen Mr. Hunter?"

He gave me a quick, apologetic look as though he knew that I had half-hoped that my story would appear to be spontaneous.

I said: "Yes, I saw him this morning. He told me that he had seen you."

He nodded and said gravely: "You know, it would have been so much simpler to tell the truth in the beginning. We are not moral judges or tale-bearers, Mr. Harrington, only the imperfect instruments of law."

I noticed with a certain malicious pleasure that even Walker was not above borrowing a phrase from Geoffrey.

I said humbly, accepting the reproof: "I know. I'm very sorry."

He dug at the white blotter with the tip of his paper-knife and said, casually, as if the answer did not greatly matter: "Had you arranged previously with Mrs. Hunter what you were both going to say to us?"

I remembered Geoffrey's line of open candour and the success he appeared to have with it.

I said: "Yes, I'm afraid we had."

As soon as I had spoken I saw the depth of the pit I had dug for myself. The room was still, quite silent except for the small muffled noises that crept in through the closed, uncurtained window. A car changed gear in the road outside, a baby wailed, and somewhere in the distance a dog was barking with a high-pitched, querulous insistence as if it had been chained up all day.

The pain behind my ribs was an inflated balloon of agony and I felt damply cold.

Walker's voice came from a great distance. He said: "Mr. Harrington, are you all right?"

I said: "Yes, I think so." The pain eased a little and my vision cleared. There was concern on his face and he had risen from his chair.

I tried to smile. I said: "It seems to be a bad bout of indigestion."

He said, as if he were really anxious about it: "You should see a doctor. These things can be troublesome."

He took a small tin out of his breast pocket and offered it to me. They were bismuth tablets; I took two and sucked them slowly.

123

They tasted clean and sweet, and they seemed to help the pain a little.

After a moment or two he said: "Do you mean, Mr. Harrington, that you had been expecting the police to get in touch with you and Mrs. Hunter? Why should you have thought that they would?"

His voice was politely bewildered but his eyes were very bright and not puzzled at all.

I said: "We weren't thinking of the police. We hoped to avoid trouble with Mr. Hunter—and with my wife."

It didn't sound very credible, but there was no hint of disbelief on his face.

He said gently: "But Mr. Hunter already knew that you and Mrs. Hunter were lovers. And so did your wife."

I said: "Yes." There seemed to be no point in trying to explain or justify.

He went on: "But they were, I suppose, unaware that you were meeting each other that night? And you didn't want them to know?"

His eyes were shining a little. It sounded a very slender story.

I said: "It was silly and wrong of us to have lied, I knew. And not very sensible. But we were very muddled—it was a difficult situation. And we hadn't thought the lie important. It had nothing to do with my brother-in-law's death."

I thought that turned the tables rather neatly. He looked a little confused as if it had not occurred to him that the lie might have meant innocence as well as guilt.

He said, loudly and almost angrily: "We think that Mr. Parry had a visitor that night."

I said: "Why should you think that?" trying to sound detached, only mildly interested.

He shrugged his shoulders and looked very eastern with his flat face and tilted eyes. He spread his long hand palm downwards on the desk in front of him.

"We're not happy about it being an accident," he said. "The medical evidence is ambiguous. It looked to me as if there had been a fight." He stared at me brightly, his eyes widening. "You didn't go to the barge, that night, you and Mrs. Hunter?"

There was a sleepy fly crawling up the biscuit-coloured wall. Its body was fat and blue, and its wings held all the colours of the prism. It climbed stickily and slowly, near to its life's end.

"Why should we have gone?" I said.

"Mr. Parry was a mischief-maker. He was an angry man and in this case he had cause for anger. He thought he had an opportunity to make trouble. Mrs. Hunter may have thought she could prevent him doing so. And you had every cause to be antagonistic towards him, hadn't you? I don't mean that you would have wished him any harm—nor that it would have been anything but an accident. . . ."

Anger seemed to be my only weapon. I said: "This is ridiculous presumption. What are you trying to do? Make me fit in with your nice, convenient little story? I'm surprised you haven't knocked me about to make me more amenable to suggestion. I thought this sort of thing didn't happen in England."

He looked unhappy, but not ashamed. He gave a small sigh. "I'm sorry, Mr. Harrington," he said.

The tendons in my neck were stiff and aching. I said: "Mrs. Hunter and I did not go down to the barge. We drove around for a little while, and talked. We had a lot to talk about. Then we went to the Goat and Compasses for a drink and then we both went home. To our own homes," I added, in case he should get any wrong ideas.

His gentle mouth drooped sadly at the corners. He said: "We have to try to find out the truth. I'm sorry if it offended you."

He showed me to the door with a sudden display of hospitality. He was a good inch shorter than me and he looked frail. He smiled wearily, and said:

"The inquest will be on Thursday. I think that some of Mr. Parry's personal possessions have already been handed over to his mother. The remainder will be available for her after the inquest."

I think I apologised before I left him. He was the sort of person who compels apology.

The things David had left behind him were undistinguished and pathetically anonymous. Mrs. Parry went through them rapidly without reminiscence or apparent sentiment like someone who is used to sorting out the belongings of the dead. She had made two piles of his clothes on the floor of the sitting-room. One pile was for clothes that were to be thrown away and the other was to go to her nephew in Porthcawl. She knelt heavily between the piles, the sun dusty on her black skirt, her thick hands folding and discarding.

"Most of it is only good for the dustbin," she said. "He used to dress so tidy when he was a boy. I can't think what got into him—wearing rubbish like this."

Nora said: "Mother, I don't know how you can bear to do it."

The socks she was mending were bundled in her lap. Her face was pale and looked thin; the sharp bones jutted beneath the flesh. Since I came in she had carefully ignored me.

Mrs. Parry said: "It's just as well that there are some of us who'll do the unpleasant jobs."

She sounded contemptuous. Nora gave a small, wounded sob and flounced up from her chair, spilling socks and darning wool. She left the room, her hand to her mouth, and banged the door. I wondered if I should go after her and decided that there was probably no point in it. I collected the scattered mending and put it back in her mending-bag. Mrs. Parry began to pack the pile of good clothes into a big cardboard box.

There were papers on the table that had been brought away from the barge in an old green attaché-case. I went through them idly; there seemed to be nothing of importance. There were bills and scribbled notes on shoddy pieces of paper, newspaper clippings and a few circular letters.

There was nothing to produce any emotion. I found an envelope at the bottom of the case that contained a series of printed lessons, part of a correspondence course on conversation. "How to Converse with Polish and Wit" was the heading of the sales blurb—the pamphlet contained a badly-reproduced photograph of a group of men in dinner-jackets and women in evening-dress sitting round a candle-lit table.

I felt sudden pity for David and shame on his behalf. I was sure that he would have hated anyone to see this evidence of his pathetic vanity. I folded the envelope quickly and put it in my pocket. It was little enough that I could do for him.

I sat in the waiting-room for three-quarters of an hour. The room was small and crowded with sallow, coughing men and women who gossiped eagerly and consistently as if it were a social occasion. I had nothing to read and there was a typed notice on the acid green wall that said we were not allowed to smoke.

The surgery was old fashioned and smelt of ether and polished leather. There was very little room between the long examination couch and the doctor's swivel-chair, so that when he stood up and moved about his surgery he did so delicately, with absurd, ballet-dancer steps, his tall body throwing an enormous, menacing shadow on the wall.

He poked and prodded at my pain and told me to put my clothes on. He sat at his desk as I did so, with his back to me, and I was ridiculously glad of the privacy, feeling as furtive as a middle-aged spinster as I pulled on my shirt and buttoned my trousers.

He said, when I was ready: "It's nothing much, Tom. A spot of duodenal trouble. Nothing to worry about yet, but you'll have to be careful. Watch your diet and that sort of thing. . . ."

He scribbled a prescription and handed it to me. "This'll help you, but it's the traditional bottle of medicine. Not much more. The diet is more important—and the way you look after yourself."

He looked at me and grinned. He had nice-eyes, he was plump and muscular and reassuring.

"Try not to get angry," he said. "It's never worth it, and in this sort of thing it's an aggravation. Probably a cause, too. You're the type who gets angry easily, of course."

I grinned back. "Perhaps I am," I said. And because he was friendly and I had known him a long time, I very nearly told him just how difficult it was to follow his advice.

Then he said, with surprising awkwardness for someone who must have been used to other people's unhappiness:

"I'm sorry about your brother-in-law, Tom. It's a nasty business. A shock for your wife and her mother."

"Yes," I said. "It was a shock." And then, lingering although I knew he was expecting me to go, only half-aware of my urgent necessity for reassurance, I went on:

"I don't really understand what happened to him. They say he fell—inside the barge—and cracked his skull. He'd had a hemorrhage and he'd fractured an important artery. They found him outside, on the gangplank. Lying with his face in the river. I saw him there. Surely, if he'd been hurt so badly, he wouldn't have been able to get up and walk?"

He looked thoughtfully out of the window.

After a while he said: "It's a difficult business. Almost impossible to tell what might have happened—afterwards, without witnesses. If someone had been there and seen him, it would be easier to be sure of a diagnose. In that sort of injury there is quite often a lucid interval between two stages. What I mean is this. A man will fall and apparently concuss himself. He may come round and appear quite normal. But if the original damage has been worse than it seemed to be—if there is a haemorrhage or a depressed fracture causing compression of the brain—he will collapse again without any warning and that's the end of it. Sometimes you can do something with surgery if you get it soon enough. More often than not, it's too late." He smiled at me kindly. "It sounds as if surgery wouldn't have helped in your brother-in-law's case, if that's what has been worrying you."

I thanked him. He looked at his watch, but not obviously. I went on because there was something I had to know.

"What did you mean when you said that it would have been easier to diagnose correctly if there had been someone there?"

There was a trace of annoyance on his plump face as if he thought he had wasted enough time on me, but it was instantly concealed by professional good manners.

"Just that the symptoms of concussion, which would be the first stage, and those of compression of the brain, which would be the final stage, are quite distinct," he said. He smiled, as if to make amends for his irritation.

"How do the symptoms differ?" I said.

He was looking at me in an odd uneasy fashion as if he were wondering what it was all about.

He said: "If someone is concussed he is pale and breathing very lightly. He would look damp and sweaty. After this condition he may recover completely or there may be a lucid interval. The signs of compression of the brain are quite different. The face is flushed, the breathing noisy and irregular. The patient would probably be throwing his head about. There's no mistake about it. Once this stage is reached it's unlikely that the patient will recover, except with treatment, and impossible, or near-impossible, for him to come round sufficiently to move anywhere under his own steam."

I said hastily, anxious now to get out of the surgery as quickly as I could: "Thank you. I didn't mean to take up so much of your time." I tried to placate him. "It's difficult, you know, being a layman. It must be a bore for you, being asked a lot of stupid questions."

Rogers said: "That's all right, Tom." His eyes were still curious. "Look after yourself, now. Don't go worrying that nice young wife of yours. She's got trouble enough without your landing up in hospital."

"I'll try not to worry her," I said.

We smiled and shook hands and he asked me about a pupil of mine who had cracked his ribs playing rugger. I walked out of the surgery and into the busy street, remembering David's purpling face and the noisy effort of his breathing. He had been near to his death and we had not known it.

And I had killed him.

For quite a long time I pretended to myself that this was all: the burden of my own, unintentional guilt. It was sufficiently heavy; it could not be lightened by accusing Geoffrey and there was, inevitably, a kind of relief in accepting the entire responsibility upon my own shoulders.

Then, because I now knew so much, I had to face the truth and go through with it. David could not have moved. Geoffrey had taken him from the barge and put him face downward in the river. He had wanted David out of the way and he had dealt with him competently and without compunction. I thought it was probable that he had guessed David was dying and he would not consider himself a murderer—only an opportunist. He would have been simply making sure. I remembered what Emily had said about Geoffrey and how he always over-reached himself, and knew that it was true.

Chapter Eleven

Geoffrey laughed at me. His teeth were white and strong and even. His laugh was merry.

"You've worked yourself into a pretty nightmare, Tom, haven't you? Why the hell should I have killed Parry? For God's sake get the thing straight. You got yourself into a fix and I came to get you out of it because Emily asked me to. It's a charming touch to accuse me of murder, now. Is this the way you usually reward people who do you a service?"

I had looked for him all over town and found him in the Fleur De Lys, dining with the Vice-Chancellor. It was a smart and expensive restaurant, the walls were lined with pleated satin, the service was silently obsequious and the carpets thick. They had been laughing together over their coffee and their skins were pink and shiny in the shaded light. As soon as they had turned to me and smiled with polite displeasure, I knew that it had been a mistake to come.

Geoffrey said: "This is an unexpected pleasure, Tom. Will you join us?"

The invitation was graceful enough, but his eyes were angry.

I said: "I'd like to talk to you alone. It won't take long."

He stared at me with an almost insolent surprise and then he apologised to the Vice-Chancellor with irritated amusement. We went to a table at the other end of the half-empty restaurant and sat, facing each other with a candle in a silver holder on the damask cloth between us. The light from the waving flame was reflected in his eyes; the pupils were dilated and made the iris look a darker and more liquid blue. He was flushed and expansive and the charm didn't slip for a minute.

He went on: "All right, Tom. So the medical evidence is confusing. But why twist it against me? You tell me that they can't be sure that he could have walked out of the barge himself with such an injury. I tell you that he did—because he must have done. When I left him, he was lying in his bunk. He spoke to me. He was apparently quite well. I'm not a doctor. I wouldn't have known that he had fractured his skull. Nor would you."

The waiter brought us coffee and double brandies. He was old and slow and the veins stood out like tender cords on the backs of his hands.

When he had gone, Geoffrey said: "What are you going to do about it? Will you go to the police?"

I shook my head.

"What then?" I did not answer, and he leaned across the table, his face supported in his hands. His voice was low and earnest and sincere.

"Be honest with yourself, Tom," he said. "Get the thing straight, once and for all. You're an intelligent man. You've got a grudge against me, haven't you? I've got everything, and you've got nothing. I win all along the line—or so it seems to you. That makes you hate me, doesn't it? Oh, don't say anything. I don't blame you, because I understand how you feel. Parry fell because you were fighting with him and he died because he fell. Whatever your legal responsibility, that makes you morally guilty. And you know it. But you can't face it. You're crawling with guilt and there's nothing you can do to wash it away. So you use me as a whipping-boy. Tom, I ask you, is it reasonable or fair?"

There was no escape from him, from his clever, persuading voice and his open, honest eyes. He was everything that I was not, clear thinking and confident, and he had me wriggling on a hook.

He called the waiter and asked for more brandy. He looked as if he were finding it difficult to focus properly. I had never seen him drunk before and was surprised to find that he talked like an evangelist.

He said, his eyes bloodshot and earnest: "Face up to it, Tom. And to yourself. Why do you want to think that I killed a man I had no reason to kill? You've no evidence that I did so. Oh, yes, I know you've got some complicated medical jargon into your head, but you don't understand it very well, and you know that you don't. You and I know why Parry died, and how. I think that if you had told the police the truth in the beginning you wouldn't now feel this need to fasten the blame on me. You're not the sort to take this kind of thing, lightly, Tom. It burdens you, eats into your soul. More than most of us you need to expiate your sins before you can be at any sort of peace with yourself. But this particular sin can't be expiated—and for you this is almost unbearable. Because you feel in the wrong, you have to blame me. And because you can't be completely sure that I killed Parry, you have to hate me too. If you had clear, unprejudiced evidence that I had done it, you wouldn't hate me. You wouldn't need to."

There was nothing in his face but friendliness and slightly drunken anxiety. I felt my hatred for him like a ball of pain in the pit of my stomach. I thought: If what he says is true, then it will never be forgiven me.

I said: "You would like to set us all to rights, wouldn't you?"

He smiled, a rueful, kindly smile.

"Forgive me for preaching," he said; "but I like you, Tom."

I couldn't take it any more. I finished my brandy and stood up.

"You'd better get back to your guest, hadn't you?" I said.

I went to the lavatory and when I came back, through the restaurant, he was talking to the Vice-Chancellor and leaning back in his chair with his thumbs tucked into his velvet waistcoat. There were two patches of bright vermilion on his cheekbones. The hair stood up spikily at the back of his head, giving him a family rakish look. The Vice-Chancellor was listening to him with a light, amused smile and he was a man who smiled rarely. Geoffrey was on top of his world.

The pub was hot and crowded; it was a wet night and there was a smell of steaming mackintoshes. I sat in a corner, on a polished oak bench against the wall, and drank one brandy after another. It was a spit and sawdust pub; most of the customers were regulars and drank beer. They played darts and laughed at each other's jokes and I felt a pariah. After the fifth brandy the sweat began to break in cold waves over my body. The pain had come back behind my ribs and I remembered that I hadn't eaten since lunchtime and that Rogers had said that it was important to eat small and regular meals.

I left my corner and went out through the swing doors, into the street. The air was cold and damp and made me feel sick-drunk. I walked down the road until I came to a telephone box. I went inside and rang Emily.

Her voice was breathless and she coughed at the other end of the line. She said that she had gone to bed, but she would get dressed and come to meet me. She put the telephone down at once, without any endearments, and I walked to the café where we usually met.

It was small and not very clean, down a back street in the poorer part of the town and we had never met anyone there whom we knew. Emily's friends would not know of its existence and the food was worse than college food, so that even the poorest of my pupils would be unlikely to go there.

I sat at our usual table in the corner. The café was empty and the waitress yawned on a hard chair by the cash desk. The place had no licence but they were allowed to bring in drinks from the nearest pub. I asked the girl to fetch me two brandies; she put the money in her apron pocket and went off with a disgruntled air, pulling her stockings straight before she went out of the door. She had fat legs, the same thick width from the ankle to the knee and she was wearing nylon stockings with black hearts embroidered up the seam.

I lit a cigarette and waited for Emily. As always, on these occasions, I was afraid. Afraid that she might have been prevented from coming, that she would have an accident on the way, that she no longer loved me. The cloth on the table was covered with cigarette ash that crawled in the draught from the window; I tried to wipe it away with my handkerchief, but the ash made dusty grey streaks on the cotton cloth.

The girl came back with the brandies. I ordered two mixed grills because the menu was always exactly the same, and we had discovered that the grill was more edible than the shepherd's pie, the roast beef or the steak and kidney pudding.

When Emily came she was wearing a cherry-coloured coat and her face was bright with happiness so that the days suddenly slipped away, and it was as it had been in the beginning when nothing had mattered except that we loved each other and were able to be together for an hour. She kissed me and we sat at the table, drinking our brandy. The waitress stood by the serving-hatch, an arm's length away, and examined the scarlet lacquer on her bitten nails with complete indifference. She had been at the café ever since we first discovered it and we were sure that she would not recognise us if she met us in the street. She had a way of looking through us as if we were insubstantial creatures, unrealities in a world where the realities were her fingernails and her bleached hair and the pile of knitting patterns that she kept beneath the serving-table.

The lift rattled up from the kitchen and she waited beside it with an air of infinite boredom. When it came to a halt she lifted the sliding door and took out our mixed grills. She brought the plates to our table, her eyes lighting glassily on the cracked wall behind our heads, and went back to her seat beside the cash desk. She took a pair of nail scissors from her pocket and began to cut her nails, the pink tip of her tongue protruding between her lips. She had a pretty, painted face and the back of her neck was disarmingly young.

Emily said: "Tom, are you well?" She looked worried, and I wondered whether I looked as ill as I felt. My mouth was dry from the brandy and my head was aching. The shoddiness of the café was suddenly sharply apparent; I was appalled that I should have to bring Emily here because there was nowhere else that we could safely meet.

I told her that I had been drinking and that I had seen Geoffrey.

She frowned. "I thought he was out to dinner. Where did you find him?"

"At the Fleur De Lys. I was looking for him."

I looked at the waitress's bent, busy head and then I told her why I had wanted to find Geoffrey. She listened silently, staring at her plate and playing with her lamb chop. When I had finished, she said: "Tom, I don't want to stay here any longer. Are you very hungry?"

The colour had gone from her face and the bright lipstick looked startlingly artificial against her skin's pallor.

"No. I'm not hungry now," I said.

I paid the waitress and thanked her for her trouble. She gave me a surprised look and a vacant smile. I helped Emily into her coat: her shoulders felt bony under her dress and I wondered if she had lost weight. We walked down the narrow stairs and into the street.

The rain had stopped and it was cool and pleasant. The people were coming out of the cinemas in a noisy, ambling crowd, their faces corpse-like under the sodium lights. I wished I had noticed the time and remembered that the local Odeon had advertised an excellent classic for this week.

I hoped that we would get across the pavement and into the darkness of the unfenced public park on the other side of the road before we met anyone we knew. Emily saw Williams before I did and pinched my arm sharply as we hesitated on the kerb. I turned, seeing the amiable, moon face and the smile of welcome that faltered into surprise as he noticed Emily. He was the senior tutor in law; we were tolerably friendly and he and his wife had always appeared to be exceptionally fond of Nora. They were a great deal older than we were, happily married and kind; I think they would have assumed that other people were as fortunate as they. I tried to smile back casually as if it were the most natural thing in the world that I should be out with another man's wife. He looked reassured, he turned and spoke to his wife and together they made their way through the crowd towards us. I took Emily's arm and steered her hastily across the road, leaving him gaping foolishly on the pavement. There had been so many other, similar encounters; I knew that when I met him next I should feel it was necessary to explain and justify, walking delicately between the twin fears of saying too much and saying too little.

In the park, the grass was long and wet against our ankles. We walked down to the river and stood looking at its liquid movement and the reflected stars. It was a light, gusty night; the pale sky was full of racing clouds, edged with silver.

Emily said: "Do you really think he killed David?"

Her voice was tired and casual. Her face was turned away from me.

I lit a cigarette and the spent match made a bright arc and hissed in the water.

"How should I know? Maybe it's as he says—that I'm so terrified of blaming myself that I have to find a scapegoat. He had no real reason for wanting him to die."

She said: "People kill each other, don't they, for quite unimportant reasons. Unimportant, that is, to other people."

The wind blew her hair in pale strands against her cheek. The moonlight made her skin the colour of ivory and when she turned to look at me her eyes were dark, pitted hollows in her face.

She said, with wonder: "Does he seem to you like a murderer?"

She was standing very still, her face uplifted, waiting for me to answer her.

I said: "Does anyone?"

She said, slowly and softly: "But, Tom, it would have been such a dangerous thing to do."

"But you see, he wouldn't have thought it dangerous. He is so sure that nothing can touch him. You told me yourself that he was never afraid."

She said: "*I* am afraid, Tom."

My head was swimming with the brandy and my pulse was fast. I said gently: "Why did you go to see David? Was it because Geoffrey asked you to?"

"Oh, yes. But I went for myself, too. There was something I didn't want Geoffrey to know. Only David could have told him."

She stopped and came close to me so that I could feel her

shivering through the cloth of her coat. She was breathing fast and her voice was high and shaky.

She said: "It was about Martin. No one except David knew. I wanted to tell you—the other night I nearly did tell you. I thought, afterwards, that I didn't tell you because I was afraid you would laugh at me, but it wasn't that at all. It was just the thing that I've always stopped at . . . ."

I said: "Go on." And she told me, in short and breathless sentences as if it were something she had hidden from herself for so long that she found it difficult to put into words.

When she had left Martin on the lawn she had been quite sure that Geoffrey was there, in the study. He had not answered her when she called out to him and the sun had been shining on the window so that she could not see very clearly into the room, but the memory of him, seen dimly through the sun's reflection on the glass, had remained with her. He had looked up from his desk, she said, and raised his hand in farewell. Afterwards, when he said that he had not been there and did not know that she was leaving the child, she had doubted the truth of her recollection, but during the weeks that she had been ill, it had constantly troubled her. And in the end she had told David about it.

She said: "I didn't want to believe it was true. I think, when I told David about it, it had seemed more like a bad dream that wouldn't leave me than something that had really happened. But then he began to question me and I was afraid it might be true."

I said incredulously: "Did you believe that Geoffrey could watch his own child drown?"

She said: "I didn't know what to believe. I had hoped that David would laugh at me."

"But you said that Geoffrey loved the child."

"In the beginning I thought he did. Most people would have done. But to Geoffrey he was a kind of shame. Do you see? Oh, he would never have done him any deliberate harm, but this might have seemed to him to be different. And I think I had always been afraid of the way he felt about Martin, which was why I blamed myself so much. I should never have left him with Geoffrey."

I said: "It sounds a delightful sort of marriage. If you really believed he had allowed the child to die, why did you stay with him?"

She said: "I don't know whether I believed it or not. At times it would seem impossible, so impossible that I thought I must be going mad. I thought it was only because I felt guilty and wanted to blame someone. Oh, Tom, don't you see?"

She caught at my shoulders and shook me as if she could compel my understanding. I put my arms round her; it seemed to be the only thing to do. I couldn't help her and because the thing had for her only the reality of a nightmare, of something seen through half-closed eyes, I think it would have been difficult for anyone to help her. The reality was, not whether Geoffrey had been guilty of his son's death; but that she had lived with the fear of it for so many years. And the fear had become, not that he had actually done the thing, but that he would find out her own, unadmitted treachery.

I no longer doubted that she was afraid of him; whether Martin's death was a cause or a symptom of her fear was unimportant. I thought, afterwards, that she had always been afraid of him; he was so alien to her that fear was engendered by bewilderment. She would never have understood Geoffrey or the delicately perverse machinery that made him tick. And she would always, instinctively, be afraid of the unknown.

She said: "These last few days I have been sure that David had already told Geoffrey—accused him, rather."

She began to cough, an uncontrolled, animal sound that seemed to tear her apart. Her body quivered between each bout of coughing.

I said: "What are you going to do?"

She shook her head and clung to me. Her voice was strained and husky. She said: "Tom, if you love me, take me away from him."

We found a hotel on the outskirts of the town, in the industrial industrict. The passages above the ground floor were lit dimly by naked, blue bulbs and the bedroom was papered with fawn roses on a geometrical trellis of bottle-green. The place smelt of cabbage and mildew and the window opened only with difficulty.

It was a big hotel, near the railway junction to the north, and they made us register separately on identical slips of white paper. It was an embarrassment we had been unprepared for, but they did not seem to be particularly suspicious when we whispered together, only bored.

We had gone to the Hunters' house before we looked for the hotel and Emily had packed a suitcase while I wrote a note to Nora. I had intended, I think, to tell her the truth; in the end I had been unable to do so and had said only that I was going away for a while and that it might be better for us both. I sent my love to Sandy.

When we got to our room Emily was shivering with cold, and coughing. Her eyes were bright and glazed and her forehead was damp. I made her get into bed and rubbed her hands and feet. I bought half a bottle of brandy from the porter and sat on the hard, high bed beside her. We drank out of thick, glass tooth-mugs and after a little while the shivering stopped and she coughed less frequently. She talked a great deal, wandering a little with fever, and hung on to my hand as if she would never let me go. She seemed completely happy; to have intruded my own private doubts and fears would have been an unnecessary cruelty.

I asked her, once, if she thought we were doing the right thing. She wrinkled her forehead at me and said: "There isn't any right or wrong, I think. Not now. You can't bring absolutes into it, can you?"

For a short time she carried me with her. She had a direct and simple belief in the rightness of happiness and love in a manner that has come to be outmoded so that she had faith of a kind where most people have an emptiness in the heart. She was able to talk about happiness as if it were not a dirty word.

But when she was restlessly asleep and I lay awake beside her, watching the lights move on the high cracked ceiling and listening to the trains shunting in the yard, I knew it was inevitable that I should fail her.

We heard his voice outside in the corridor, talking to the chambermaid. He was speaking loudly as if he thought her deaf; she mumbled something in answer and then came the swift sound of his feet and his knock on the door.

We had had breakfast and were almost ready to leave. In another ten minutes he would have found us gone. Emily was still coughing and she had eaten very little, drinking several cups of black coffee because she said her throat was hurting her. She had laddered her stocking and was changing into another pair; her bare feet on the worn rug looked rosy and cold. When he knocked on the door she was standing with the stocking in her hand; she looked at me and stiffened into stillness. Her face was naked with surprise.

I went to the door and opened it. Geoffrey came in, the bright beads of rain still clinging to his hair. His raincoat was wet in dark patches on the shoulders. He was breathing lightly, and quickly like a man in a hurry. His face was bony and exhausted, his eyes had no expression in them at all.

He said: "I've come to take you home. It's raining. I've brought your mackintosh." And he handed it to her.

She took it and put it on the bed.

He said: "You'd better finish dressing. Do you want me to wait outside?"

His voice was as weary as his face. A vein twitched in the hollow shadow beneath his eye. He behaved as if I were not in the room.

She said: "I'm leaving you. I'm going away with Tom."

He said: "Are you sure of that?"

The muscles of her face had contracted and become rigid.

She said: "I'm sorry, Geoffrey."

His voice was suddenly and surprisingly venomous.

"You say that you're sorry when you tread on a man's feet in the Tube. Not when you ruin his life."

I was startled, not by the anger because that was expected, but by the apparent unhappiness behind it. It was more than hurt pride or indignation; it was evidence that, after his fashion, he loved her. I had not believed him capable of love; now, looking at Emily's white, shocked face, I knew that she had not believed it either. And it had taken the ground from beneath her feet.

He said: "Have I treated you so badly all these years? Have I been such a bad husband to you?"

I wondered for a moment whether it was deliberate pathos, assumed for a purpose, and then it seemed unfair and self-excusing to think like that and I was ashamed.

She said nothing. Her eyes did not leave his face. Then she shook her head slowly and looked at me, sad-eyed, waiting for me to help her.

I tried. I said: "I'm going to take her away."

He looked me up and down, and then he smiled.

He said: "Well, Tom, I suppose I must wish you joy. Are you going to marry her?"

I said: "I hope she will marry me."

He nodded, his eyes considering me. I tried to stand still and not shift under their light, grey gaze. Then he sat down on the bed, fumbled in his raincoat pocket and began to light his pipe, his skin reddened by the match's intermittent flare. He cupped his beautiful hands carefully round the bowl and the flame like a man who is used to lighting a pipe out of doors.

Emily turned her back on us both and began to roll on her stocking.

He said casually: "What about Nora, Tom? Does she know what you are doing?"

I said: "No, I haven't told her."

A train rattled and banged its way across the viaduct. The cheap, glass ash tray danced on the bedside table.

He said, contemptuously joking: "Would you like me to do it for you, Tom? She'll have to know. And you aren't very good at picking up your own broken pieces, are you?"

I said: "I'll tell her when she has to know."

He grinned over his pipe. "How long can you avoid decision. Tom? Shall I start divorce proceedings against Emily?"

She was standing beside me. Her shoulder was very close, but she was not touching me. I could hear her breathing.

I said: "There's no hurry, is there?" And I heard her sigh softly. "I shall have to talk to Nora, try and explain to her. Her brother has just died; it would be a cruel moment to walk out without a word. I am responsible for her."

The room was silent and washed with yellow light the colour of fog. It was as if the sun never came into it except dimly, through a cloud of smoke.

Emily stirred beside me gently, like someone waking from sleep. She walked to the bed and picked up her mackintosh. Geoffrey helped her to put it on, guiding her arms as if she were a child. He looked very tall.

He said: "Have you packed your suitcase, dear? Did you have anything else?"

She said something, but her voice was so low that I could not hear. She didn't turn until she was at the door. Then she began to cough again and leant against the lintel until the spasm passed, her face screwed up and scarlet, her shoulders huddled into the raincoat. Then she looked at me across the width of the room.

She said: "Poor Tom." Her voice was gentle and empty of complaint.

They went out together and the door closed behind them.

Nora smiled at me from the pillows. She looked pale and the skin was puckered round her eyes. There was a dark line on her lips.

She said: "I'm sorry, Tom. I've had a bad head. Worse than I've had for a long time. Mother sent for the doctor and he gave me an injection."

There was faint pride in her voice. She showed me the light bruise on her arm where she had had the injection and asked me to sit beside her and stroke her head. She closed her eyes while I did so; in spite of the pain she looked ten years younger and unworried as if in her temporary illness she had found a safe retreat. She put up her hand to my face and held it against my cheek. She had tiny hands, so thin that the fragile bones showed through the flesh. She had always been very vain of them, and I could never understand why; I had always thought them ugly and now I found their touch repellent, like the touch of a cold bird.

I must have made some sort of movement because she opened her eyes and looked at me.

She pouted like a little girl, and said: "You don't have to stay with me if you don't want to. Mother will give you lunch downstairs."

I said: "But, Nora, I want to stay with you," wanting suddenly to make up for everything, most of all for not wanting to be with her, for not wanting to touch her.

She frowned a little as though she disbelieved me. Then she said: "You aren't going to leave me, are you, Tom?"

Her voice was affectedly childish; it was the voice in which she asked for a new dress, a visit to the theatre.

I said: "No, I'm not going to leave you. Now you must rest and get well."

She looked at me with a more adult anxiety and said: "Tom, you do love me, don't you?"

I said, drearily conscious that I was committing myself finally to the lie: "Yes, of course I love you."

She sighed and closed her eyes again. Her dark lashes were long and curled; they looked moist against her cheek.

She said sleepily: "You know, if you'd left me, I think I'd have killed myself."

She was asleep quite quickly. She always slept heavily and well, although she complained continuously of not doing so. When she was breathing regularly I left the bed and closed the curtains against the pale, mid-morning sun. I went downstairs to have lunch with Mrs. Parry.

Chapter Twelve

I said: "Why did you fetch me?"

For a moment he didn't answer. His profile, etched in the reflected light from the headlamps, was intent on the road in front of him. In this way, with most of his face lost in shadow, the high narrow bridge of his nose and the receding slope of his forehead stood out more sharply than normally as in a caricature.

At last he said: "Because if she wants anyone, it will be you."

He glanced at me briefly, with sad anger, and turned back to the windscreen and the road.

I said, because I had to say something, not yet realising the monstrousness of my own part: "Why did she do it?"

"Have you no idea?" he said, and after that we did not speak. He drove the car at a steady sixty and I huddled coldly in my overcoat, turning up the collar against the wind that whipped through the open window.

The starlight was pale in the sky and once I looked at my watch. It was five o'clock on an autumn morning and Emily was dying. If she were not already dead.

Geoffrey had found her about an hour and a half before he had come to fetch me. He had tried to telephone, but my number had given the engaged signal. I discovered, afterwards, that Sandy had been playing with the receiver and had left it off the hook.

They had gone straight home after leaving me at the hotel. Emily was not well; her temperature was slightly above normal and her cough was troubling her. She had said that it was only a cold and she would not see a doctor. Geoffrey had left to go into the town and when he had come home, in the late afternoon, he had found her listless and exhausted, coughing in a chair by the fire. He had persuaded her to go to bed and she had done so, saying she did not want any dinner. She would take a pill, she said, and try to sleep; her cold would be better in the morning. Geoffrey had insisted that she had some whisky and given her a stiff drink in a tumbler. A little later he had made a warm drink and taken it up to her. She said she was sleepy, the whisky had given her a headache and she did not want to talk. He had left her and gone downstairs to his own cold supper and an article that he particularly wanted to finish.

It had taken him longer than he had expected; it was for a Sunday newspaper and in an idiom to which he was unused. It was well after midnight when he went upstairs to bed in his dressing-room. He did not want to disturb Emily, and he had not gone into her room. Once in bed, he found it was impossible to sleep. The wind had got up and was rattling the window sashes; after reading for something over an hour, he was still wide awake. He remembered that Emily kept her sleeping pills in the bathroom cupboard and he decided to fetch them. When he reached the bathroom, they were not there.

He said: "I supposed she'd decided to take one after all—she'd said, when I gave her the whisky, that she wouldn't. I was a bit worried. You aren't supposed to take those things when you've had alcohol. There have been one or two nasty accidents that way. . . ."

I said, foolishly, because it was not important now: "I didn't know she hadn't been able to sleep."

He said: "Did you really think she would be so unaffected?"

The door of Emily's room was ajar and banging in the wind. He was quite sure he had left it closed. When he opened it farther he saw that her bedside lamp was lit, and the wind was blowing through the wide-open windows, billowing the curtains. A couple of small ornaments had been knocked off the dressing-table below the window; one of them was an ash-tray made of heavy Venetian glass that must have made quite a lot of noise when it fell. He was faintly and distantly surprised that Emily had slept through the racket; he closed the sash window with a slam and turned to look at the bed.

She was still breathing, but so lightly that the bedclothes above her barely moved. There were tiny beads of moisture on her skin and her lips were cyanosed.

He said: "The bottle was beside her, on the small table. At first I thought it was an accident. The whisky, you see, and then getting drowsy and having the tablets beside her, in the bottle. It is the thing they are always so careful to tell you not to do—the first dose makes you muzzy and you forget that you've taken it. But there was no chance that it was bad luck. The bottle was quite empty and this morning it was almost full. I noticed it when I took my shaving things out of the bathroom cupboard. I remembered I was angry because she had put it there and not locked it up in the medicine chest. It seemed the least she could do if she were going off with another man—to leave my house in order."

I wasn't in the mood for his particular brand of joking.

I said: "Was she all right when you left her?"

"Would I know? We were being very polite to each other. I didn't think she was particularly unhappy."

He hesitated, and then he went on as if in justification, to talk of his own complete bewilderment. She had a capacity for enjoying life, he said, even when it dealt harshly with her; she must have suffered beyond bearing to take such a way out of it.

He had felt her pulse and then he had rung the doctor. He had arrived within ten minutes and brought the district nurse with him. It was already too late to move her to hospital; the loss of time would be more important than the extra care they could give her. He and the nurse had done what they could; in the end he had told Geoffrey there was very little hope. And Geoffrey had come to fetch me. I never really understood why he did that.

When we reached the house, all the windows except one reflected back the morning redness of the sky. In Emily's bedroom a light shone out; I saw a shadow move across the closed curtains.

A frightened maid in a Jaeger dressing-gown opened the front door before Geoffrey had time to find his key.

She said: "The doctor's been asking for you, sir," and scuttled away, the metal curlers bobbing on her neck.

The sickly, sour smell met us as we went up the stairs; in the room itself it was almost overpowering. There was a rectangular table by the bed, the kidney dishes and rubber tubing half-covered by a white towel. I tried not to look at the table. I didn't want to know what they had done to her.

The doctor was sitting on a chair by the bed, writing on his knee. He had come out without his tie and the collarless shirt, buttoned up to his neck, made him look like a labourer. The nurse was holding Emily's wrist and watching her stopwatch. She was a very young girl, plump, with healthy cheeks. She looked at, us shyly as we came in and laid Emily's arm back on the bedcover.

Emily was lying on her back and very still. The honey-coloured hair was soaked with sweat and tangled on the pillow. Her eyes were closed and the mauve flesh beneath them seemed to be without bones. She was as white as the linen on which her head lay.

The central light in the ceiling was on and its glare was merciless. Under it both Geoffrey and the doctor looked old and tired. I stood between the bed and the door while Geoffrey talked to the doctor. They went over to the window and whispered together. The nurse took a cloth from the table and wiped Emily's forehead. She did it gently with raw, young hands.

We were in the study when she died. The nurse came running down the stairs to tell us as if the moment of death were important. Her kind, round face was flushed and upset; she was very near to tears.

It was about seven o'clock in the morning and outside, in the street, there was the clipping of the milkman's horse and the rattles of his cart. We switched off the electric light and drew back the dark curtains as if in recognition of the end of a vigil. Geoffrey looked unshaven and dirty, his suit was crumpled as though he had slept in it and his face was deadly tired. He went upstairs with the nurse and then, a little later, I heard him talking to the doctor in the hall.

When he came back into the study he said: "There was nothing

148

we could have done. There wasn't, at any point, anything we could have done."

He stared at me with his prominent eyes. "The doctor says the police will have to know. He telephoned them as soon as he knew that she was dead."

He gave me a cold grin. "Apparently they wait until they're sure a suicide has been successful before they inform the police."

He was very pale and there were deep lines on either side of his thin mouth. He said, in astonishment: "I would never have believed it. She wasn't that sort of woman."

I thought how odd it was that we should speak of her, already, in the past tense.

I said: "Did you have a row?"

He looked at me dully. "I suppose so. We both said a lot of things we didn't mean. Or perhaps we did mean them. I don't know."

I said: "She was afraid of you."

"Afraid? Why should she be afraid?"

"Because she thought you were a murderer."

As soon as I had said it, the absurdity became apparent.

He looked startled, at a loss. Not guilty. I asked him about Martin. Cautiously, because it was already retreating into fantasy.

He got up and went to the window. The sun streamed in from a high blue sky.

"I thought it was Parry's story. Anyway, not hers. Not ultimately." There was a brittle silence and then he went on, more easily: "After it happened she was in an appalling state. She blamed herself so much for leaving the child—much more than anyone else blamed her. For a little while she was out of her mind. When she was in the nursing home she accused me of murdering the child; she was in a kind of delirium. The doctors said it was the normal transference of a guilt too great for her to bear. They were very embarrassed about it when they told me.

"Then she was well enough to come out of the nursing home, and I thought it was all over. She never spoke of Martin to me; once or twice I tried to make her, thinking it might do some good.

But she always reacted so violently that I gave up doing so. Then the rumours started—I never dreamed that she might have started them. . . ."

"What were the rumours?" I said.

He shrugged his shoulders. "Nothing definite. Pretty untraceable—even if they hadn't been, it was a difficult sort of business to take any action about. The worst and most damaging was a story that the housemaid we had at the time had said she was sure I hadn't left the study. There was a small pantry on the landing at the top of the first flight of stairs. It was a big house, you see, too big for the domestic staff we could afford, and this place used to be the butler's pantry where he brewed the coffee after dinner. We kept some china there, and the silver. The girl was polishing silver, she said, throughout the time in question and she would have been bound to see me if I had come out of the study, because the door was immediately opposite the bottom of the stairs and in full view of the pantry. The girl was a thief and an habitual liar—while Emily was in hospital I dismissed her and sent her back to her family in the south. When the rumours started, I tried to trace her, but the family had moved. They were itinerant pedlars—a graceless lot. But there seemed to be no good reason to go to any more trouble. We were leaving the country and not likely to return. If I had thought that Emily believed the stories I would have made more effort. But I trusted her. I thought she had too much sense of loyalty."

He sounded injured and surprised. I said: "In the circumstances it would hardly seem to be a matter of loyalty."

He said: "But she can't have believed it. Besides, she had only to ask me."

"And you would have convinced her that you were innocent. You always convinced her of everything, didn't you? Perhaps, for once, she wanted to work it out her own way."

His eyes were like stone. He said: "There is no need to be impertinent, Tom." And I nearly laughed in his face, seeing him for the first and only time in my life as pathetic, standing on his silly dignity, unable to bear censure.

Then the moment passed and I hated him again, because his pompous, schoolmaster's reproof had been successful so often before and would be so again.

I said: "Did David tell you that Emily believed that you had killed your son? If she had believed it, then other people might have believed it too. And David didn't care about the consequences to himself; he didn't value his life very highly. It would have needed no more than a hint in a newspaper column to have ruined your career for you."

His face was blurred and grey. He made a blind, rough movement towards me and then stopped, his hands held out in front of him because the door bell rang.

Both of us stood quite still. Then the maid said, from the doorway: "Inspector Walker has come to see you, sir."

Walker said: "Did you think her the sort of woman who might take her own life?"

His voice was sad and diffident; he looked tired.

"No," I told him. "No."

He was less composed than I had ever seen him; his narrow hands moved restlessly on his knees. His uneasiness was painful.

He said jerkily: "I saw Mrs. Hunter yesterday morning. She telephoned and asked if she could come to see me."

She had come in a taxi and she swayed a little as she walked into the police station as if she were drunk or ill. She had made up her face heavily and falsely; her hand must have been shaking because the lipstick had slipped over the edges of her mouth and the mascara was thick on her lashes, gumming them together in dark, sticky points. She was wearing the sable coat that Geoffrey had bought her and diamond clusters in her ears. Her hands were heavy with rings. Her voice was high and clear and hard, for she had to hide her fear, and that was a good way to do it; to wear her expensive clothes and to look and sound like a bitch. It had not fooled Walker; he spoke of her with an odd and gentle pity.

"Poor lady, she wasn't quite herself. She said that she had come to tell me what happened on the night Mr. Parry died."

He had said that David died. Not that he was killed. It was a very distant kind of relief.

She had gone in order to protect me. It was her last gesture of love; she must have known what it would cost her.

He said, surprised: "She seemed to have the idea that we suspected you. And, of course, we did, as you must have known. Though not of Mr. Parry's murder. I may say that what she told me tallied quite remarkably with what we thought must have occurred."

He went on, sadly and thoughtfully: "Not all of it, of course, because she tried to do the impossible. She said that she went to see David Parry on his barge because he was threatening to make trouble for her husband, and she thought that she could persuade him to desist. She tried to pretend that she was a very bad kind of woman. I didn't believe that. She said that you saw her car and followed her there. Then there was a quarrel that was not of your making. Mr. Parry attacked you and knocked you down. She pushed him and he slipped on a bottle and fell. She was very insistent that the fight was not your fault and that you did not touch him, even in self-defence. When it was obvious that he was badly hurt she telephoned her husband and asked him to come to the barge."

He looked at me. "Is that how it happened?" he said.

I could have denied it; she was dead and she had been ill when she made her statement. But my life was no longer worth defending; I stood helplessly in its ruin and told the truth.

I said: "Yes. Of course we tried to hush it up. I don't know what happened afterwards when I left the barge."

He looked at his hands. "She said that Mr. Parry died then, before she joined you in the car. That she asked her husband to say nothing to you." His eyes were bright and moist. "I think she wanted to protect him also, perhaps she loved him too. If it had been possible she would have taken the entire guilt on her own shoulders. This is the part of her story that we cannot believe—it is against the medical evidence. It is unlikely that death could have come so quickly."

He rose abruptly from his chair and stood in the centre of the room, staring in to space.

He said, with sudden and quite unexpected violence: "She was crucified between you."

The words dropped like stones into the room. He looked, as soon as they were spoken, angry and abashed as if he had been tricked into a display of emotion.

"Mr. Harrington," he said, "what happened yesterday—between the three of you?"

He seemed not in the least like a policeman. I told him that Emily and I had gone away together the night before, and that we had intended it to be a final departure. I told him what had happened in the early morning and how Geoffrey had come to the hotel and taken Emily away with him.

He sat down slowly, crushed and shabby in the big leather chair. The clipped Midland voice was harsh.

He said: "So she went home with her husband, not because she chose to, but because you found that you could not leave your wife?"

I think that he had meant it to sound like an accusation, as if I had betrayed a trust.

"Yes," I said. "I suppose so."

Curiously, I wanted to explain, to vindicate myself in the eyes of this common little man, but I knew that he would know any defence to be as shoddy as paper.

"Do you think," he said, "that this final rejection by you—because it was final, wasn't it?—might have forced her into suicide?"

I told him that I didn't know, and I knew that this was true. I had no idea what it might have meant to Emily; at the end I had thought of myself and not of her.

He said: "She had sunk everything in you. All her life she had been sure of nothing. With you and in you she had found herself and a kind of peace. Without you there was emptiness. She had only despair."

His cheeks were darkly flushed as if he were ashamed of the things he was saying. I did not think to wonder at the springs of percipience and imagination she must have touched in this dry man; I only thought that it was as if we were talking about someone I had never known.

Then he smiled, suddenly and sweetly, and said: "I'm sorry, Mr. Harrington. This is a kind of torture for you. But I have a reason."

I said slowly: "If you are trying to make me say that I thought she was the sort of person who could kill herself, I can only say, even now, that I would never have believed it. I know that I was wrong, but even knowing that she did it in the end, doesn't make it believable for me."

He said: "I thought you would say that. Indeed, I hoped you would. You see, I agree with you."

Chapter Thirteen

I handed in my resignation three days later. There seemed to be nothing else to do. We sold the house in Sanctuary Road to a neighbour whose son was getting married in a hurry. I found a job in one of those small, free-education schools that exist for the spoiled children of the fashionable intelligentsia. They had wanted an assistant master for some time and were glad to get anyone. The pay was bad but a cottage went with the appointment, and the countryside around the school was high, purple moorland, the winds blowing, sharp and bitter, inland from the grey North Sea. It would be a change from the lush green of the river valley and the sluggish air.

I remember very little about the whole of that time except that the days were crowded and yet seemed to be barren. The nights were long and dark and empty; I slept rarely and then only from exhaustion, waking with a furred tongue and a throbbing head. The pain in my stomach seldom left me; for most of the time it was there, a constant reminder of my body's weakness until I became used to living with it and it no longer worried me. The days passed and brought no solution, only acceptance of despair.

A few, blurred pictures of Nora remain with me. In the days after Emily's death she tried to enfold me with love, believing, or wanting to believe, that I had returned to her because I loved her. When I rebuffed her with unintentional silence or merely by forgetting that she was there, she withdrew into her own world and, I think because she thought I wanted it, tried not to bother me. When I went to bed she lay, unmoving and still, beside me. So still that she must often, have been, awake and feigning sleep.

The house was cleaner than it had ever been. It smelt of furniture wax and antiseptic; the fire was always welcomingly bright in the polished grate. One day she took down all the curtains and washed them; I found her, in the late evening, ironing them in the kitchen. She looked flushed and tired, but she made no complaint and only smiled at me in the determinedly bright, apprehensive way that had become a habit with her as though I were a tyrant of whom she was afraid. When I was in the house she came and went on silent feet like a timid ghost so that her unnatural quietness, her attempts to deflect attention from herself, became an additional burden of condemnation. Mrs. Parry went to live with her sister because there would be no room for her in the cottage. I think she was glad to go; even she had grown taut and strained and uneasily silent as though the situation had defeated her funds of private malice and she could not have dealt with it in any other way.

Only Sandy was unaffected; he sang and swooped and shouted round the house and in the tangled garden, riding his new bicycle along the shabby pavement so that when he was there life assumed a sort of temporary reality and purpose. He loved the new cottage, the low, smoke-blackened ceilings and the bare wooden stairs that were enclosed in a cupboard at one end of the stone-flagged kitchen. There was a big uncleared garden and he and I spent the end of the autumn days cutting down the crowded trees and overgrown bushes, and making bonfires that were his abiding joy. He fed the broken branches into the crackling smoke with a tense and private pleasure, absorbed in the moment in a way that brought a temporary heart's ease, watching the small, shut face and the sudden child's smile as the branch he had carried to the fire flared into sparks that hissed on the damp wood. We planted bulbs for the spring in the cleared ground and scythed the grass that had grown long, like hay.

There were old apple trees growing in the wide ditch that marked the garden's boundary. Most of the fruit was finished and fallen, but there was one tree left with late hard clusters still clinging to the branches. The apples were small and sour and not fit to eat, but Sandy gathered them like a squirrel and stacked them in the garden shed. He plagued Nora until she bottled some of them to please him, but the rest rotted into a brown, sweet-smelling mess on the concrete floor of the shed. I meant to bury them in case his feelings should be hurt, seeing them lying there and wasted, but when I forgot about doing so and he found them later, spoiled and rotten, he said they were a lot of nasty rubbish and kicked them with his boot, forgetting his careful gathering and the days of eager work.

I bought him a mongrel puppy, a wild, squirming black creature, half Labrador. It was a little over six months old and we walked him for miles across the moors when school was over, training him to carry sticks and bring them back to us when we had thrown them. He was an engaging dog with a lolling, wet tongue and clumsy paws; at night he slept on Sandy's bed, whimpering in his sleep.

Sandy grew brown and well in the bright, cold air. His legs became sturdy and covered in pale, silky down. There were moments when, watching him run before me and seeing his laughing face as he turned to cry out some new discovery, I thought that some kind of permanent healing was taking place within me. But when he was in bed and sleeping, and the wind sang down the chimney I knew it was an illusion.

For the weeks after we had first come to the cottage, Nora had not sat with me in the evenings. I did not know whether it was from embarrassment or genuine preoccupation, but I was glad of the respite from the sense of guilt that her presence brought me. She made curtains for the cottage, using her sewing machine on the kitchen table because it was more convenient there and the light was better. When she was not sewing she seemed to find endless small jobs with which she did not want my help, and I sat by the fire in the sitting-room and tried to read, hearing her movements about the house and longing for her to go to bed. We lived together like a pair of strangers with a barrier of silence between us.

In the end, the silence became brittle. She began to join me in the evenings, bringing her sewing and her magazines to the chair on the other side of the hearth. Her movements were gentle and timorously shy; when she spoke it was haltingly, as though she were afraid of offending me. It became impossible to keep up even a semblance of reading; whenever I looked up, she was there, her head bent over her work apparently absorbed in it, but I could feel the tenseness of her body like an electric current in the room.

One day I went into the nearest town to order paper and books for the school. When I came home she had cooked a special supper and bought a bottle of wine. She had laid the table with a lace cloth and candles and we had a chicken. She was wearing a red silk dress that we had bought together two years before, and she had curled her hair and made up thickly so that she looked five years older than her age. She was brassily bright; it was an uneasy moment for a celebration.

When we had finished eating I wanted to wash up, but she said brightly that this was a party and we would leave the dishes until the morning. So I sat stiffly and alone by the fire in the sitting-room, waiting for her to bring in the coffee.

When she came, she carried the tray with care. With the coffee was a half-bottle of brandy and the balloon glasses that belonged to a set we had been given as a wedding present.

She put the tray on a low table and held the bottle out to me.

"Look, Tom," she said. "We've been gloomy long enough."

I tried not to disappoint her with pretended pleasure, smiling at her until my mouth felt fixed and hard. She turned out the centre light and switched on the soft reading-lamp, settling herself at my feet with her silk skirts swirled about her. The heat of cooking had made her make-up run a little so that her skin looked drawn and unnaturally lined. She toasted me with her brandy, raising her glass and smiling at me with sudden, artificial coyness so that I knew, immediately, the purpose of the party.

At first I wanted to laugh. Loud, hysterical, idiot laughter. And then I wanted to run away, out of the room, before we could humiliate each other further. But it was impossible. I stayed, with Nora sitting at my feet, and we played out the farce to its inevitable end.

She drank her brandy quickly and then another as if she wanted to give herself courage. Her brightness grated like a nail on a blackboard. She gave me a brave, jangling smile.

She said: "Tom, it's so lovely to be alone here, with you. I am so grateful."

It sounded wooden and long-rehearsed. I knew how much effort it had cost her.

I said: "I hope you will be able to be happier."

She twisted round and fondled my knee. "I am sure we could both be happier," she said. "Tom, I love you so much. Can't you love me a little?"

I said: "Silly one, of course I love you."

She stared at me. The brightness had gone and her eyes shone with despair. She got up from the floor and flung her arms around me, pressing her body against mine. She was trembling. I kissed her and released her gently; she stood up in front of me, her hands flung out like a suppliant.

She said: "I'm not ugly, am I? Or wicked? Couldn't you be happy with me?"

Terror rose up and engulfed me. I felt for the words to stop her, to stop her degrading herself in front of me. Oh, God, I prayed, let her stop before it is too late, before she learns to hate herself for ever.

She pressed her small hands to her breasts, smoothing the silk over their childish roundness. Her eyes were wild and hopeless and her mouth trembled.

She said: "You used to love me. You don't have to love me now if you can't love me. But I'm a woman, aren't I? Not the one you want, I know, but I'm here and I love you. Won't I do? Do you find it so terrible to touch me?"

I put my hands over my ears, trying to shut out the sound of her high cracked voice and her desperate unhappiness. I think that I said I was sorry, over and over again because there was nothing else that I could say, nothing else that I could do for her.

At last she ran from the room and the door of the cupboard stairs slammed behind her. I heard the creak of the springs in the room above as she flung herself on the bed. I stayed by the fire until the red cinders fell on to the hearth beneath, knowing that she would never forgive me or herself for this, knowing the agony of shame that would be with her always and that the responsibility was mine and mine alone. At some point I might have done something, averted tragedy. Now there were no more chances; the pattern was rigid in its mould.

After a while, I went into the kitchen and washed the dishes. I threw the empty wine bottle into the dustbin and put the brandy bottle at the back of a cupboard. At least she would not be faced in the morning with immediate reminders of her disaster. It was all I could do for her.

The next two days were a nightmare. She would not look at me or talk to me, and when, she did there was something in her face that was much like hatred. Even Sandy seemed to sense the tension in the house; he came home late from school and went out again immediately after tea, going to bed when he was told silently and without fuss, so that the cottage seemed quiet and cold and empty.

On the morning of the third day, life intruded. The paragraph in the northern edition of the London paper was small and on an inner page. Geoffrey Hunter was to be tried in two weeks' time for the murder of his wife. He had been arrested, six weeks after her death, about a fortnight after I had left the town.

I suppose that I should have expected it. In the months before we left there had been sufficient indication of the way things were going. But at the time I had been aware only that she was dead; nothing else had mattered or had had any reality. I had known that the inquest had been adjourned at the request of the police, and I imagine that at some level or other I had known it to be significant. I was too obsessed with the fact of her death to be much concerned about the manner of her dying; even if I had thought then, as I did not, that Geoffrey had killed her it would not have seemed to be of very great importance.

Walker had been to see me twice before I left. Looking back now, on those interviews, I realised that I should have known the way the wind was blowing. He had asked me about Geoffrey during one of our conversations and whether he had been jealous of me, and bitter against Emily. I had said that I thought not; that if he had felt anything it would have been insulted pride of possession. Walker had smiled then and said that it was not always the obvious emotions that were the dangerous ones.

We had not, on the whole, talked much about Geoffrey. Mostly he had wanted to know about Emily, seeming to be obsessed with her so that I had grown tired of his dry, gentle voice asking questions that it was a torment to answer. I had gone on repeating that I would never have thought her capable of suicide, feeling that it must be for him, as it was for me, a constant wonder that anyone so unlikely could have taken her own life, not realising then that he was using it as evidence to build up a case in his own mind for murder. Even if I had known, I am not sure that I would have answered very differently.

But remembering came later. At the time there was only shock like the shock of cold lake water on a blazing day. At first there was relief because if Geoffrey had killed her, then I had not; if he had murdered her, then I was not as guilty of her death as I had believed myself to be.

The second reaction was one of simple disbelief. Geoffrey could not be, and was not, a murderer. I reminded myself that I had believed him guilty of David's death and that Emily had been sure he had allowed his only son to die; I tried to persuade myself that this was something different. That even if he had been, in a way, responsible for David's death and for his son's, that it was not the same thing. In Martin's case he had not taken any deliberate action; in David's, he was merely hastening a process because it suited him to do so. But he could not have killed Emily, not Emily.

Then I knew that my reasoning was false and the inability to believe was in my own mind. That when I had believed him to be a murderer; it had been in the irresponsible realms of speculation only. That I would never, as Geoffrey knew, have gone to the police even though my suspicion, had been ten times as well founded because that would have meant translating fiction into reality.

But now that had been done by other hands than mine. Geoffrey had been arrested and the entire, be-wigged and solemn panoply of the law set in motion against him. He was still innocent because he had not yet been proved guilty, but his innocence was difficult to credit because he was awaiting trial.

In the morning I had a letter from Geoffrey's solicitors, saying that they wanted to see me in case they should want to call me as a witness for the defence.

I went to see Geoffrey in the prison. His solicitor told me that he had asked to see me and that he had already made arrangements for the visit. There was no decent way of refusing and I was, I think, too bewildered to do so. The solicitor was a small man with an open, ruddy face and an air of being a farmer. He wore country clothes and his office was tidy and uncluttered in a way I had not expected. He asked me questions about Emily, the same questions that Walker had asked, and seemed to be disappointed by the answers. He hinted, when he had finished, that it was unlikely that I should be wanted at the trial. Then he asked an office boy to call a taxi to take me to the prison; he smiled and said that it would be put down to expenses.

At the prison, they showed me into a bare, long room with a table down the centre that was topped by a barrier of wire mesh like the counters in General Post Offices. There was a high barred window at one end of the room and there were chairs on either side of the table. The room was very clean and smelt of antiseptic, like a hospital.

Geoffrey looked as he had always done; except for the fact that his suit was not as well pressed as usual he might have been dressed for the day in London. Only in his face was there any perceptible change; he was more lined than I remembered him, and there was a dark shadowed hollow below the cheekbone that had not been there before. His hair was fair and shining, and looked cropped and naked round the ears as if they had cut it in prison.

He grinned at me. He said: "Tom, I'm sorry to have dragged you into this silly muddle."

At first I thought it was an act, the conventional behaviour expected of a gentleman, but as we went on talking I knew that he believed it. It was a silly muddle, no more, no less. And his confinement and his trial only the disagreeable preliminaries to his release. I do not remember how I felt; perhaps astonishment and anger. I know that sympathy and anxiety were removed and replaced with dislike.

He told me that they had arrested him when he came home from a party.

"An official party," he said. "I couldn't have avoided it. And when I came back, there was the Inspector waiting for me with a policeman. An unpleasant ending to a not-altogether unpleasant evening. He's a stupid little fellow, that policeman. I told you he was on the look out for promotion."

I said: "But why? What reason have they got?"

He shrugged his shoulders and his eyes smiled at me. "That on the evening of whatever the date was I did feloniously procure and administer to my wife a noxious substance with malice aforethought. Or some such jargon, Tom."

I said: "But she killed herself. You told me so."

"I made her some chocolate," he said. "They found some of the barbiturate in the sediment at the bottom of the cup. The capsules the stuff was in were quite pleasant to take—a sort of jelly coating that slips smoothly down the throat. I imagine they argue that she wouldn't have bothered to mix them up with the chocolate; they would have been just as easy and pleasant to take as they were. I am not altogether up in the case for the prosecution, but we had a row, before she went to bed, and I suppose that the maid was there, and heard us."

I said: "But there has to be a motive."

He looked at me steadily and I saw, with surprise, that there was a white line round the coloured part of his eyes. I had seen it in ill and very old people; I think it is called the senile arc. I knew, because I had read it somewhere, that it could be found in people of thirty and over; somehow it was unexpected to find it in Geoffrey as if one had not thought to find in him any sign of decay.

He said: "She loved you, Tom. She loved you so much that she left me to go away with you. She only came back to me because she had nowhere else to go, and because you did not want her. It might be a reason for suicide, Tom, but it might be a reason for murder. No one likes to be cuckolded or betrayed in any other way. At some point or other the civilisation cracks."

He was smiling, a sure and confident smile. "I don't believe they have a very convincing case, Tom. You and I know, more than anyone else, how much she loved you and how much she lost when you sent her back to me. She was a very simple creature; she believed in the judgment of the heart. She had never been unfaithful to me before, you know. There had been other men but it had all been innocent. It was emotional release she was looking for, not sexual fulfilment. She was not a particularly passionate woman, you know."

I said, with a dry throat: "What about David Parry?"

"Parry? No, I don't think so. Oh, I know that you thought she had been his mistress and maybe she didn't bother to contradict you. You were very jealous, Tom. You wouldn't have believed in her innocence. Only I did that. And so I was the only one who knew what it meant to her when you went back to your wife."

His eyes were moist. "I would not have killed her, Tom. She was my wife and my responsibility."

He looked haggard in the pale light that came through the barred, unclean window. I tried to remember that he was a hard man and that hard men were almost always sentimental. It was the opposite side of the same coin.

There was a small silence while he looked at the window and I stared at his profile, wondering why I had found it worth while to hate him. And wondering why he had wanted to see me.

Then we talked for a little about the trial. He had, he said, an excellent counsel. He did not seem to be concerned about the final outcome; his main theme was his own complete astonishment that they had arrested him. I do not think that at any point he felt any doubt or dread. Something had gone wrong because of a stupidity; it would, in time, be righted and those who had caused him trouble would be made to suffer for it.

Before I went, he said: "Did she never give you any idea that she might do this? Did she say nothing?"

I shook my head.

His eyes narrowed suddenly so that they looked very pale and shining.

"She did not even write to you? I should have thought that, at the end, she would have written to you."

I said: "No," and he sighed. Not as if it were the one hope he had clung to, but rather as if it were tiresome of me to have no corroboration of the fact that she had taken her own life. It was impossible to feel any particular pity for him because even here, in prison, it seemed that he had everything on his side.

It obviously seemed to him a ludicrous farce that he should be deprived of his freedom, even though it was only a matter of time before it was restored to him.

We were not allowed to shake hands. When the time was up the policeman told us so and another policeman came through a door on the opposite side of the room to me and led Geoffrey away.

When I felt the prison I left ill and sick. The pain had come back behind my ribs with more force than usual. I went to an A.B.C, and bought myself a cup of white coffee. There was skin like glue on the top of the liquid and I burned my lip. I felt only half-alive as if I were moving through cotton-wool.

Chapter Fourteen

The doctor said: "When do you get the pain? After you have eaten, or before?"

His face and Nora's floated above me, looking like the balloons at children's parties with grinning, spherical features painted on their emptiness. The pain was almost unbearable and, in a way, welcome.

He said in a jolly, fatherly way: "Well, we won't need to send you to the butcher's this time. A few days of rest, care with the diet . . ."

They went out together and I heard their voices through the closed door.

"It's often anxiety as much as anything else, Mrs. Harrington. It's frequently a cause and often a hindrance to recovery. Has he had any particular worries lately?"

Her voice faded down the wooden stairs with the clatter of her heels.

"Oh, no, Doctor. He's not been particularly worried. But he's always been highly strung and a new job, you know, is always a worry."

I thought: So she can't tell the truth, not even to a man who is always hearing secrets. Respectability was too necessary, the desire to hide corruption with a sepulchre.

I lay there, between white sheets, looking out at the high, moorland sky through the window and the white scudding clouds. I told myself: Nothing is over, presently I shall get better and life will begin again. Nothing is ever irrevocable; there is always hope. The door opened slowly, and I thought it was Emily coming in. The moment expanded into hours; she was a long time coming through the door, but soon she would be with me, in the room, and I would see her.

Nora came in with the tray and I was angry because she wasn't Emily. For a moment I wanted to ask her where Emily was, and then I remembered that she was dead and I had been wrong about there being hope.

Nora had brought me a glass of milk.

"You must drink it now, while it's warm. I'll make you some more in two hours' time. You have to have it all through the night. I think it would be best to get a Thermos and then you can set the alarm clock so that you wake up."

She plumped up the pillows behind me and made up the fire in the poky, old-fashioned grate. She was very brisk about it and talked all the time in a loud cheerful voice.

"Will it be all right if I take Sandy to see Joan Mansfield this afternoon? I won't be long—I may not even stay to tea. I rang her this morning and promised to take her some of my bottled cherries. She's such a nice woman and it would be nice for Sandy to play with her little boy. He's got lots of lovely toys—she has her own money, you know."

I said: "She certainly doesn't get it from her husband. I shouldn't think he makes much out of the school."

I was sorry for Mansfield. He had the shy, apologetic look of the convinced failure and he was terrified of his nagging, clever wife.

She sniffed. "I shouldn't think he'd make money anywhere," she said. "Joan's too good for him. Did you know she was at Girton? I'm so glad we've met her. It's lovely having someone about who talks your own language."

I wondered if her enthusiasm would survive the first snub. I had seen her like this before, looking for friendship with the over-anxiousness of the lonely, trying to win people with pathetic presents. I wondered whether Joan Mansfield would make her a target for her contemptuous wit and hated her in prospect.

I said: "Go along to your tea. But I'll be glad if you don't stay." Trying to soften the blow of an unwelcoming reception.

She said: "Perhaps I won't stay, then. I'll take the cherries and come straight home. Would you like to read?"

"No. I'm too tired, I think."

She looked at me with concern. "Are you sure you don't mind being alone, even for a little while? Will you try and sleep? The doctor said you ought to sleep."

"I'll try," I said. I felt, suddenly, unwilling to let her go; her presence shut out the emptiness and the futility. But we had nothing to talk about; there was no reason to ask her to stay.

I said: "Enjoy yourself. The walk will do you good."

When she came back, I knew that she had not been asked to tea. She said she had been worried about my being alone so long, but her mouth was dragged down at the corners and her voice was nervously light.

When she had put Sandy to bed, she came to sit with me, eating her supper by the bed. I saw, for the first time, that there was grey in her hair and new lines round her mouth. I thought: This is what I have done to her. And this is only the outward sign, the decay that shows.

In a little while she looked at me shyly and said: "Darling, why don't you talk to me about it?"

"Talk to you about what?" I tried to smile at her.

She floundered. "You're terribly unhappy, aren't you? If only you'd let me help you. I want to, so much. After all, I love you."

I said: "Can you love me? I shouldn't, if I were you. I'm not much good to anyone."

She leaned towards me, her face flushed and earnest.

"Darling, you mustn't talk like that. Please don't talk like that. It doesn't do any good. Perhaps I used the wrong word, maybe love has too many interpretations. But we're adults, not children. We're fond of each other. We can make life easier for each other. Will you let me try?"

I wondered what magazine she got it from. And then, I thought: Perhaps love isn't the wrong word. Perhaps this is love, this thing you feel for the people whose trust you betray, this desire to protect what you have already destroyed.

I said: "I don't deserve it," feeling the weak tears in my eyes.

Her face was lit with missionary zeal. She said: "You *are* fond of me, aren't you, Tom?"

"Of course I'm fond of you." I thought drearily: There is no end to this, I am committed now. Seeing in front of me the treacherous bog of easy, sentimental affection, the conventional covering of lives without grace or joy.

She kissed me on the forehead and then on the mouth. It seemed like the confirmation of a lie.

I found the letter four days later. I was downstairs, in the sitting-room. I was not supposed to work, but there were letters that had to be answered and bills to pay. The desk was a small bureau with a sliding compartment in the flat part of it which we used very little because when you were sitting at the desk you had to clear the papers away before you could get at it. Inevitably, it hid a collection of rubbish that we never had time to tidy up and throw away. This afternoon, I opened it before I started to write, looking for the last receipt for the rates on the house in Sanctuary Road. I had promised, when we left, to send it to the present owners and I had forgotten to do so. They had written to remind me about it.

Nora was in the room and when I found Emily's letter she was standing beside me. It was lying there unopened among the letters and the receipts and the bills. For a moment I felt, absurdly, pure delight. I took it with the eager hands of a miser. And then, with the stiff envelope in my hands, I began to be afraid.

Nora gave a deep indrawn sigh. I looked at her and her face was scarlet.

She said, gabbling: "It came after she died. You weren't there, I knew it came from the village by the postmark. I thought, now it was all over, we could be happy again. It was like a hand from the grave."

I said, wondering: "Why didn't you destroy it, then?"

She began to cry as a kind of safety measure, fumbling in her pocket for a handkerchief.

"I meant to. I know it was wrong, but I meant to put it in the fire. Then we would have been finished with her. I had it in my hand and you came into the room when I wasn't expecting you. I was standing by the desk—I'd been looking for something when the postman came, and I went back to the desk to close it after I'd picked up the letter. So when you came in, it was the easiest thing to do—to drop the letter in and shut the desk. For a little while I was going to take the letter out and burn it, but there was always someone in the room. And then we moved and I forgot about it."

I said, and it felt as though my tongue were weighted with lead: "Don't worry. I expect I would have felt the same way."

Her face glowed as though I had done her an unexpected kindness. She said: "You're not angry?"

I shook my head, wary of trying to comfort her further, knowing that the only way we could live together was to keep the barrier between us and not break through it with fumbling occasional affection.

She hesitated. Her eyes slid away from my face and fixed on my chest. She said, with appalling, sad humility: "You'll want to read it, won't you?"

And she went out of the room and closed the door softly behind her.

The room tilted sideways and I put my head between my knees. My knuckles grazed against the side of the bureau; I forced myself to sit upright and open the letter.

It was short. It was written in the violet ink she habitually used, on very stiff paper with deckled edges. It made her seem very young, somehow, as if she were a girl in the sixth form writing her first love letter.

MY DEAREST TOM,
This is the last letter I shall write to you and it is to say that I have never loved anyone in my whole life as I do you. I am

only sorry that it has to end like this. My poor, poor darling. It will be a terrible time for you, but now you must only think of the future and of Sandy and try not to be afraid any more. Try to forgive me, because I love you and love doesn't come to an end even if people do. There is so much that I would like to say and I don't know how to because just now words seem so inadequate, and I was never very clever with them. God bless you and watch over you, my love.

EMILY

The room was cold. I was alone in an unsafe place. She loved me. She loved me more than anything else, more than I knew and more than I deserved. She was sorry for me. And I had failed her.

There was a time after that when nothing seemed real except my own, terrible responsibility. I remember that after everyone was in bed and the house was dark, I got up and tried to pray. I knelt by the bed like a child gabbling his good night prayer. Desire struggled in my body, too formless to express. It was only just beyond my reach like a familiar word that is temporarily forgotten, but that you are sure the next moment must reveal. I repeated a prayer that I had learned at school, trying to instil into the formal, empty words a meaning that they must once have held for others if not for me. And then the monstrous hypocrisy struck me like a blow. How could I ask for comfort when I had betrayed her? The transient need was almost gone and I saw myself with contempt; a tired man searching for the remembered comfort of a father image.

I turned on the light by the bed and read the letter again. She had said: "It will be a terrible time." Not, "it is." She had said good-bye. Geoffrey had known she would write to me at the end. I had not thought her capable of suicide and I had been wrong. She had believed, with the simplicity of a child, in her love for me; there had been no alternative.

Then I remembered that Geoffrey was on trial for her murder

and a little time after that I saw the postmark. The letter had been posted the day after she was dead.

The light grew gradually brighter at the end of a dark tunnel. When she wrote the letter she had been making a gesture, a gesture she wasn't sure she intended to carry out. She wrote the letter and left it, perhaps on her dressing-table. Geoffrey had seen it, either before he killed her, or afterwards. He had posted the letter to me, perhaps not thinking about the postmark, perhaps believing it would be indecipherable. At first I wondered why he had bothered to post it and why he had not given it to the police. Then I knew that it was as Emily had said; he always over-reached himself. He was so sure that her death would look like suicide that he could afford to risk my not producing the letter. And it would look more plausible if she had posted the letter to me before she killed herself; it was unlikely that she would leave a farewell letter to her lover where her husband would find it after she was dead.

I wondered if he was surprised when I had not shown the letter to the police. When he mentioned it, in the prison, it had been, perhaps, a gentle prompting.

It was only in the morning that the reasoning seemed hollow; I clung to it because there was nothing else that I could do.

Some time during the evening, Nora came into my room. She said, with carefully averted face:

"Tom, in that letter—did she say she was going to kill herself? Shouldn't you give it to the police?"

I said, flinging it in her face, forcing myself to be brutal because it was the only way to silence her:

"No. It wasn't a suicide letter. It was personal—just a love letter."

Geoffrey's trial lasted for three days. I was one of the last witnesses they called for the prosecution. I do not think I realised at the time how heavy was the weight of evidence against him.

The lights in the court were very bright. When I turned away from the judge I could see the public benches with the rising tiers of blank staring faces. All of it had a cardboard quality, like a stage set.

I do not remember what the prosecuting counsel looked like. He had a gentle voice. Counsel for the defence was a small man, thin to the point of emaciation. He had a white face and a savage mouth.

He said: "Mr. Harrington, you say that you are sure Mrs. Hunter would not have committed suicide. Let me refresh your memory a little. You had both decided to break up your homes and go away together. A decision which one assumes was neither casual nor temporary. And yet you rejected her. You rejected her in front of her husband, the man she had left for your sake. And so she had no choice but to return home, unwillingly, with her husband. Can you not see that this was a situation that might well have been intolerable for someone far less sensitive? Can you still say, under oath, that you do not believe she would have killed herself?"

I think that the prosecution objected at this point and that the objection was sustained. Certainly I know that I did not answer the question and the sharp, ferret-like features were replaced by the bland, anonymous face of counsel for the prosecution.

"As I understand it, all that you said to Mrs. Hunter was that you could not leave your wife immediately. Is that so?"

"Yes."

"And what did she say?"

I felt, although I could see no one clearly, that all the eyes in the court contained contempt.

"She said that she was sorry."

"Did she appear despairing?"

"I did not think so."

And then my evidence was over. I saw Geoffrey during the brief time I was in court, sitting in the dock with the warders on either side of him. He looked distinguished; he was listening to the evidence with complete, detached absorption. From time to time there was a look of faint amusement on his mouth.

The trial ended that afternoon. I left the court because I could not bear to stay there. I sat in a café and waited for the verdict. It was a raw, foggy day, the people hurried by the wide window with their scarves across their mouths. In the café they served sweet, strong tea and enormous, sticky buns with a few lonely currants in them. The customers were mostly workmen from the factory; they left the sodden stubs of cigarettes floating in the brown dregs of their tea.

In the end a newsboy came into the café with the evening papers. The verdict was in the stop press. To-morrow there would be photographs in most of the papers. He had earlier caught the public imagination as a romantic figure; on the last day of the trial several women had been removed, weeping, from the court. This evening there was nothing but the bare fact, in blurred, black type. He had been found guilty of the murder of his wife, Emily Maud Hunter. He had been condemned to death.

A fortnight later there was an appeal and when the appeal failed, I went to see Walker. I had known all the time that I would have to go; I had been waiting, perhaps, for a miracle.

They let me in at once. I had the impression, as I walked in the door and saw his bright, smiling eyes that he had been waiting for me.

Of course he did not say so. He pretended to be surprised. He was smoking a cigarette and because I had not seen him smoke before I was surprised to see that his fingers were covered with nicotine stains.

I said: "She wrote to me before she died."

"Yes?" he said, leaving the word to trail in the air like the tobacco smoke.

"It didn't reach me. My wife didn't want me to have it. I found it in the desk where she had hidden it."

He gave me no help. "Well?"

"She said good-bye. She said she was sorry it had to end like this. It was a farewell letter."

He smiled with his mouth. "Did she say she was going to kill herself?"

"No."

"People usually say so. Have you got the letter?"

I said: "No. I burned it."

He looked at me across the width of the desk. There was a thoughtful expression in his eyes. "A pity," he said. "Why didn't you bring it to us before you destroyed it?"

I told him about the postmark. I said: "It seemed to me to be conclusive."

"Ah," he said; "but one mustn't jump to conclusions." He stubbed out his cigarette and emptied the ash-tray fastidiously into the wastepaper basket as if the dirty ash offended him.

He said slowly: "Why should you think he posted it? There was a maid in the house, wasn't there? It was one of her duties to collect the mail which was put out on the hall table and post it. At night and midmorning. She might have missed the late post." He grinned suddenly as if it were amusing. "No proof, of course. She didn't remember whether there was a letter to you among the mail. We asked her."

"For God's sake," I said. "What can we do about it?"

"Do about it?" he inquired with what seemed to be genuine astonishment. "Do about it? Mr. Harrington, he has been convicted by, a jury of his peers. The case against him was pretty strong, you know. The only person who doubted it was Mr. Hunter himself. He was quite sure that he was safe and that no one could touch him. He was so sure that he didn't bother to wipe his fingerprints from the bottle and from the cup. And perhaps, as you suggest, he posted his wife's letter. They had quarrelled. There had been trouble about Parry's death. And there was her story about the child. No proof, of course. Not allowable evidence. But sign of a troubled background. As you remember, I saw Mrs. Hunter on the day she died. She was a fine woman; there was a lot of life about her. I don't believe she committed suicide." He looked at me sharply. "What evidence can you put against this? A letter you say you have destroyed."

I said drearily: "She loved life so much that she was capable of leaving it."

"I don't understand you, Mr. Harrington."

"She wouldn't have been able to endure the framework of living if there was no reality there."

Quite suddenly his eyes were very kind.

"You can't let it alone, can you?" he said. "You know, you mustn't mistake your own sense of guilt for a legal responsibility. It confuses the issue."

I remembered that Geoffrey had once said much the same sort of thing to me.

I said: "Render unto Cæsar." And he nodded slowly and smiled at me.

I met Walker once more, after the execution. I had gone back to the university to pick up some papers I had left with my successor.

I was walking down the main street and I saw Mrs. Foster, Stevie's mother, on the other side of the road. I crossed, dodging the buses, and went up to her.

I said: "Hallo, Mrs. Foster. How is Stevie?"

I don't suppose she had ever cut anyone before in her life. She reddened and walked on as if she hadn't heard me, leaving me with a stupid smile of welcome dying on my face. So I didn't see Walker until he was standing next to me. Curiously, he appeared to think it an occasion for festivity. He asked me to have lunch with him and we went to the Fleur De Lys. It was a busier place in the middle of the day than in the evening and we were lucky to find a table. We had a bottle of burgundy with our lunch, and afterwards the same aged waiter brought us brandy in balloon glasses.

We talked about the weather and about my job. We told each other a few faintly dirty jokes. And then I asked him about Geoffrey. I had to know.

He said: "He was sure, right up to the end, that he would be set free. Some of them are like that, you know. They can't believe it. One wonders, sometimes, if there is ever a moment when it becomes real."

It was an unemotional generalisation. Geoffrey was not exceptional. . . . He had gone to his place of execution incredulous to the last, unable to believe that this should be the end of him, that for once there was no way out.

We didn't talk for a while and then I became aware that Walker was watching me. His eyes were shining and his brown face looked ageless. He was a stranger, suddenly, and I said, because it is easier to say these things to a stranger:

"Is it my fault?"

He was diffident, in spite of the brandy. Or perhaps because this was a social occasion and he needed the authority of his desk.

He said: "You take it too hard, Mr. Harrington. Doubt is inevitable. On earth, no one can decide the ultimate responsibility. Not even you, with your letter. The letter you didn't burn."

He smiled, and we finished our brandy silently. We left the restaurant together and, standing on the pavement, said good-bye to each other.

I went to college and found the senior common room empty. I stood by the open window and looked out at the quad and the winter sun, moon-pale and low in the sky.

I knew I was tired. I took out Emily's letter and read it. It had become sharp, tangible evidence that I had failed her. The worst and heaviest burden is always the burden of other people's love.

There was a tray of dirty coffee cups on the table. I burned the letter over a saucer, lighting one match after another because the paper was thick and difficult to destroy. When there was nothing left but dark, charred ash, I took the saucer to the window and emptied it. The cold wind caught some of the dust and tossed it high, like small, grey, birds' wings. The rest blew back in my face.

THE END

Printed in Great Britain
by Amazon

74964512R00111